Kee-To, Iron Hand

Kee-To Iron Hand is the one Sioux leader white soldiers have never been able to corner or capture. His daring raids and uncanny ability to avoid being behind bars have made him a priority for the cavalry officers to find and jail. But Kee-To has the blood of fighting ancestors and their mystical whispers to him to keep him free. He would rather die than let the horse soldiers pen up his people behind fences under guard. That climatic battle finally came in the Siouxs' mass exodus to reach Canada and safety. Can he prevail one last time?

Kee-To, Iron Hand

Art Isberg

A Black Horse Western

ROBERT HALE

© Art Isberg 2020
First published in Great Britain 2020

ISBN 978-0-7198-3075-4

The Crowood Press
The Stable Block
Crowood Lane
Ramsbury
Marlborough
Wiltshire SN8 2HR

www.bhwesterns.com

Robert Hale is an imprint
of The Crowood Press

CHAPTER ONE

The low log building stood in the black of night under an ice-sheathed half moon, surrounded by a land covered in deep winter snow. A pair of military guards wrapped in army blankets over their uniforms stamped out small depressions in the freezing blanket of white as their booted feet ached, turning numb with cold. Inside the darkened structure no fireplace crackled to life-giving heat. No coal oil lamp lit the shadowed gloom to show the six Indian chiefs held there. Each was given only one skimpy blanket against the bitter cold. The six huddled together in one corner, talking among themselves in low whispers, fearing what the horse soldiers would do to them next.

One of the six turned away from the hushed conversation, beginning to dig with bare hands against frozen ground and rocky soil. He hated the horse soldiers, and all white men for that matter. He'd sworn not to let them decide his fate while the pounding heartbeat of his Sioux ancestors pulsed through his veins.

'Kee-To, what are you doing?' One of the older chiefs

turned to him.

'I am leaving this place. No soldier will hold me here to hang. If you are wise, all of you will follow me from this place.'

'No soldier has said that,' another Indian spoke up. 'If you try to run away, we will all pay with our blood.'

'Your memories lie to you, my brothers. Do I have to tell you of our warriors who kicked at the end of cavalry ropes in this same prison? Open your eyes. These white horse soldiers are our enemies and always will be!'

'Even if you dig your way out, they will ride you down and bring you back. Every step you take will be written in snow. You cannot escape.'

'You are my brothers and always will be. But you have already forgotten why we came here. They said it was to talk of peace. Do you believe two guards at the door are for talks of peace? It was a trap to bring us in. If we cannot lead our people, the women, children and old men will have no choice but to do what white soldiers order them. They will be loaded on his smoking iron horse, like sheep, and taken far away from our own lands, to live in reservations and never know the freedom we have always lived by.'

'But the Great White Father in Wash-ton told soldiers to bring us here to talk of peace. He is chief of all white men. He would not lie to us.' A third chief challenged Kee-To.

He kept digging until his fingers bled red, with no more feeling. Without stopping, he answered back. 'The Great White Father is leader of all white people. He cares not for us, but his own brothers. What will it take for you to learn that? Never believe anything any white man tells you. Their tongues wag like a dog's tail. All they say are lies.'

An hour of painful digging finally saw the last boulder removed supporting the corner logs, to a rush of freezing cold air from outside. Kee-To straightened up, turning back to his friends, one last time. Taking a bloody finger, he drew three straight lines across both cheeks in his personal sign of war paint.

'Will any of you now come with me? This way out is freedom to ride and fight as we always have. To stay is to die.'

None of the shadowed five uttered a single word. Kee-To only stared back before sliding into the tiny depression, with a final warning. 'I do not think I will see any of you again until we ride together in the Spirit World. Good bye my brothers.'

The moment the young Sioux warrior chief disappeared, the remaining men began replacing dirt and stones, smoothing out the hole until it looked natural again. One of them finally spoke in a whisper. 'I think Kee-To will be killed before the sun rises far. The horse soldiers will track him down like a running rabbit.'

'He is foolish to do this thing,' another added. 'He thinks only of himself and not his people.'

Outside the log prison, a frozen, black sky was ablaze with icy stars. Kee-To straightened up, hesitating a moment in shadows, knowing the blue-coat guards were just around the corner. The tall outline of snow-laden trees stood only yards away. He moved toward it at a crouch, his knee-high deerskin boots already beginning to soak through with icy wetness. Now he had to move fast. At a low crouch he started away shielded by the trees, silently as a ghost.

At the front of the prison, the pair of military guards walked in slow circles, pulling the wool blankets higher around their shoulders against the bitter winter night. One man turned a moment, looking back at the corner of the building. 'Did you hear something?' he asked.

'Yeah, it was my feet beginning to freeze solid. You got any tobacco, I need a smoke?'

'I've got the makin's, but you'll have to roll your own.'

The second blue coat poured tobacco into cigarette paper, licking the edge to seal it before lighting a match. 'You ever wonder why the captain's got us out here? It makes no damn sense, to me. These Indians can't go anywhere even if they did get out with all this snow.'

'I don't think Captain Stodlmeyer is too worried about what we think. He's in a nice warm bed with a pot-bellied stove turning cherry red while we're out here, half freezing to death.'

At first dawn, an orderly woke the Captain Austin Vance Stodlmeyer with a start.

'What in God's name do you mean, one of the Indians escaped last night!' He sat straight up in bed, grabbing for his clothes on the night stand next to him.

'I don't know, sir. That's all the sentries told me when they did a head count.'

Stodlmeyer pulled on his pants and boots, muttering under his breath and standing to shuck into his shirt before running both hands through light brown hair.

The orderly helped him into his jacket and hat, adorned with a woven gold head band and cross swords insignia on the front.

'Now let's find out what in hell this is all about. I want to talk to those Indians myself. And go get Sergeant Merchant. I want him for an interpreter too if I need one.'

'Right away, sir.' The private saluted, quickly exiting the bedroom.

Inside the log prison, the captain stood looking down at the seated chiefs, before turning to Merchant. 'A couple of them do speak some English don't they?' he questioned.

'Yes sir, they do,' the sergeant nodded, 'Running Horse, stand up.' Merchant pointed at the old man. 'Captain Stodlmeyer wants to talk to you.'

The old man slowly came to his feet, his dark eyes meeting the captain without blinking, both men sizing each other up.

'Kee-To is the one who escaped isn't he? How did he get out of here without my guards seeing him? I want a straight answer, you understand?'

'I . . . do . . . not . . . know.' Running Horse took in a long, slow breath.

'Don't give me that. You and the rest of these Indians were right here. You're not blind, are you!'

'We . . . sleep. Maybe he . . . fly away like . . . bird. Kee-To is medicine . . . man. He has . . . many powers.'

'Many powers, my foot. Merchant, who else can I talk to? I'm not wasting any more time with this fool.'

The sergeant pointed to another chief, motioning

him to get up. 'This is Buffalo Horn. He speaks some American, too.'

'All right, let's try this again. You heard my question to your friend. How did Kee-To get out of here? And I want an answer that makes some sense. Not any more of this Indian, mumbo jumbo.'

'Kee-To can do things . . . no white man . . . can. He Spirit Warrior.'

'If I don't get a decent answer out of any of you, you'll get nothing to eat or drink until I do. You understand me? I'll let you sit in here and starve for all I care. I will not let a bunch of savages get away with this!'

'Sir.' A soldier suddenly came through the door. 'We found footprints in the snow out back. The escapee must have went out that way, sir.'

Rushing outside, Stodlmeyer and Merchant along with several soldiers followed the footprints into the trees, seeing the tracks leading away.

'I've got him now.' The captain's voice rose with success. 'Let's get to the horses, and run him down. I'll have him back here before breakfast and make an example out of him the rest of them will never forget!'

The line of blue-clad cavalrymen rode away from the log-walled outpost at a gallop, snow flying from their horses' heels, bursts of steamy air from their nostrils. The lead tracker, a Mexican–Indian half-breed known as Big Hair Ozona, led the line, his shoulder-length black hair flying out from under his cavalry hat in the freezing morning air. His eyes never left the snowy ground, nor did he utter a single word the first mile as he followed the footprints of the running Sioux warrior. Up ahead the timber thinned noticeably over rock-strewn ground. Big Hair slowed his horse from a steady gallop to a trot, then a slow walk, reining the animal in circles while he leaned out over the saddle trying to puzzle out the vanishing prints. Captain Stodlmeyer rode up alongside him.

'Why are you slowing down?' he demanded.

Without looking up the tracker mumbled something Stodlmeyer couldn't understand. 'Speak up. I can't understand whatever you're saying.'

The brown-faced man finally looked up, locking eyes with the captain. 'He gone now,' was all he said.

'What do you mean, he's gone? Keep on following him. Let's get to it!'

'No tracks over rocks,' he pointed. 'Maybe he go any direction now.' He swung his arm out in a wide arc, over the brilliant white landscape.

'Then we'll circle ahead until we're off these damn rocks and pick him up again. He's afoot. He can't be that far ahead of us. I won't waste time letting him get any farther. Get going, Big Hair. That's what the army is paying you for!'

Three hours later the riders were back in the outpost stabling their horses, while Captain Stodlmeyer walked into his office, shucking out of his heavy blue coat and gloves. At the heat from the pot-bellied stove, he warmed icy hands, massaging them until feeling came back. The metallic taste in his mouth was the bitter taste of defeat. If the Sioux escapee hadn't made it to rocky ground, he'd have him back here in prison, under guard, right now. It rankled him he'd been outsmarted by a savage like that. Even worse, he'd have to write that in his daily report ledger. He had to be found at all costs, to face these new charges of escape and erase the stain on Stodlmeyer's record. He went to his desk, sitting down and pondering his next move. In a moment he had a new idea. He'd call in one of the other chiefs to see what he might be able to learn about where Kee-To could be running to.

The chief Hawk's Eye was brought in to stand before the captain, while two armed guards stood behind him. The old man stared emotionless at the officer, wondering why he'd been brought here.

'I'm told you speak some American, too. Is that correct?'

'Maybe . . . little bit.'

'All right then. I want to know more about this Sioux chief called Kee-To. I'm told his full name is Kee-To Iron Hand. Is that true?'

The chief nodded, but did not answer this time.

'First, I want to know how he escaped. One of you must have seen something?'

'I sleep. No . . . see him . . . go.'

Stodlmeyer leaned back in the chair, trying to gauge the honesty of the answer, as Hawk's Eye stared back at him, offering nothing more. He decided to change the line of questioning. 'What about this odd name of his, "Iron Hand"? What is that supposed to mean?'

'It say . . . Kee-To always has . . . gun in hand.'

'It does, huh? Well he doesn't have one now. He left here unarmed.'

'Soon . . . will have. No white man . . . can catch . . . him. Medicine, too . . . strong.'

'We'll see about that. He won't get far in this weather. We'll likely find him frozen stiff as a board under some brush pile. We're not done tracking him. I'm going out again tomorrow. Before I let you go, I want to know where you think he's gone to?'

Hawk's Eye stared back at the captain. For just an instant, Stodlmeyer thought he saw a change of expression flash across the old man's face, then it was gone so quick he wasn't sure any more.

'Well, do you have an answer?'

'Can . . . white man . . . fly?'

'What do you mean by that?'

'Kee-To . . . is . . . Spirit Warrior. He flies . . . like bird. You no . . . find him.'

The captain ordered the guards to take the chief back to the log prison with one final order. 'I don't want any of these Indians given anything to eat until I get more answers. I'll starve the truth out of them, even if it takes all winter!'

The running warrior knew the horse soldiers would not give up looking for him, riding farther out each day as they failed. Kee-To was in a race against time not only to save himself, but his village and possibly even the entire Sioux Nation, as he'd been doing these last three years. He could not read a book on military tactics nor match the increasing numbers of white soldiers or their weapons steadily coming into these ancestral lands of his people. But the white invaders had already found themselves on ground they knew little about. Kee-To knew every ridge, canyon, waterhole and game trail as far as the eye could see. He would use every advantage of his natural world to keep back the invasion threatening his people and their way of life.

Far north of the tall log stockade walls he ran on like a dark shadow, staying in thick timber where the snow had not drifted so deep. His buckskin boots were nearly frozen to his feet, except for the lining of dry grass he'd stuffed into them. The cavalry blanket taken with him when he escaped hung over his shoulders like a cape tied around front, with just enough warmth to keep him from freezing to death. He was heading for an old hideout he'd used as a teenager when he first discovered it while out hunting alone. If he kept up this pace, he could reach the cliff-walled chain of mountains in two more days.

The hideout's fractured rock face was lined with cracks and crevices, except for one small opening a man could just squeeze through. A large boulder concealed its entrance into a small but hidden oval clearing of grass fed by a small spring. In its center, he'd built a small bark-walled teepee strong enough to keep out rain and snow. Inside the A-shaped structure, he kept a change of fur winter clothes and knee-high buckskin boots laced around the tops. A cache of dried nuts, berries and venison were held in leather bags hung on the walls. The most prized possession of all was the pistol and rifle his father had given him just days before he was captured and taken away from their village. Two more deerskin pouches held cartridges for each weapon. Kee-To never saw his father again, only hearing he'd been tried and hanged by a jury of white horse soldiers.

He quickly stripped off his frozen clothes. Naked to the skin, he wrapped a bearskin cape over his shoulders before building a crackling fire, sitting to soak in its life-giving heat. As he warmed, he remembered the words of warning his father, Battle Spear, had told him years ago. He'd said the white man meant to subjugate the Sioux and all other tribes before forcing them to leave their ancestral lands on their smoking Iron Horse. Kee-To stared deeper into the hypnotic dance of flames, search-ing for hidden answers how to fight the horse soldiers and win victory for him and his people. Out of the snap-ping, twisting tongues of gold and blue, a far away whisper came to him saying he must first go back to his village before anything else. He must warn them of what was coming, then tell them how he meant to stop it. He nodded slowly, still transfixed. He'd heard the message from the Spirit World. Tonight he would sleep warm and safe. Tomorrow he'd start for the village with renewed vigor.

At dawn, Kee-To awoke to smear bear fat onto his moc-casins, making them waterproof. Shouldering a small skin pack with only enough food to make the journey, he strapped on the .44 caliber pistol and picked up the Winchester rifle of the same caliber. With the bearskin cape over his shoulders, he struck out for the village three days away. His proud face and prominent features were framed by black shoulder-length hair tied in two braids in front with silver amulets near the ends. A pair of white, black-tipped eagle feathers formed a high V tied in the hair at the back of his head. Heavy deerskin pants and shirt protected him from bitter cold as he ran. But no war paint lined his thin, dark face. That would come later, after he reached his people.

Days later, several Sioux teenage boys were out gathering firewood when one looked up to see Kee-To striding out of timber. 'Look!' one pointed, dropping his arm load. 'Kee-To is back, but he comes alone!'

The youngsters eagerly ran to meet him with questions about what had happened at the soldiers' outpost, but he held up his hand stopping them. 'My words will be for your fathers at council tonight when I speak of it. They are not meant for the ears of young boys.'

'But Kee-To, we are already old enough to fight,' Little River objected. 'I already have a bow and reed arrows I made myself. No white soldier can come into our village without feeling the cut of my arrows!'

'In time you may get the chance to use them when you can ride and shoot straight. For now, keep those thoughts in your head. If the day comes when I am no longer here, it will be you and your friends, grown to warriors, that must take my place.'

His powerful words stunned the boys into silence, watching him stride away toward his teepee. When Little River found his voice again, he blurted out his feelings.

'No warrior can take Kee-To's place as chief. I hope he does not think I meant that. He is our greatest warrior of all, and always will be!'

That evening the entire village filled the big timber-built council lodge situated at the far end of three dozen buffalo hide teepees. The lodge was the meeting place for warriors and elders to discuss major issues and plans affecting the entire tribe. Usually, it was for the men only. But tonight was different. Kee-To had asked that all his people be allowed to hear what he and the other chiefs had experienced at the hands of the soldiers. A large fire pit in the center was lit, warming the lodge as everyone came in. Men, elders and warriors sat up front in a large circle around the fire. Women, old people and boys sat behind them, their concerned faces lit in shadows. Kee-To waited for the lodge to fill completely and everyone was seated. One of the elders stood ordering quiet as a woman at the back hushed her crying child.

Kee-To began by walking in a slow circle around the fire, looking into the faces of each councilman as he passed. Then he spoke. 'What I have to tell all of you is not good. Five other Sioux chiefs are being held in the horse soldiers' prison right now. Only I escaped to be here. We were told the white men wanted to talk of peace. That was a lie, as we should have known.'

A murmur of concern went around the ring of seated men until one warrior dared to speak up. 'How did you escape, when the others are still there? Their people need to hear from them, too. Did they not try?'

'They did not. They believe to escape would only make more trouble for all of them that stayed. I did not. They would not believe me when I told them they would be hung, as other Sioux leaders have been. I was not going to let that happen to me.'

'If the soldiers have the leaders of all five tribes, the

17

Sioux Nation has no one to guide them in war against these white men,' one of the elders spoke up.

'Yes, but that will only be if the chiefs remain captives. I have a plan to set our brothers free for the fight that will come. That is one reason why I called for this meeting of everyone.'

'What plan? How can we fight against all the white soldiers and their guns? Their numbers grow and never stop.' One of the younger warriors shook his fist.

'Hear my words, my brothers.' Kee-To held his hand high, silencing the worried whispers circling the big room. 'The soldiers must take our chiefs to their white man's court far away. They will do that using their smoking Iron Horse. When they move them, I and our warriors will be waiting to stop them and free our brothers.'

One of the elders finally stood up in protest and concern. 'Our few rifles and pistols cannot stop their Iron Horse. It is too strong. It has no flesh. It does not bleed!'

'That is true, but we do not have to take the entire Iron Horse, only the car that holds our people. I believe I know how to do that. I will take twelve warriors with me to strike our Sioux hand at the heart of the soldiers.'

'Twelve braves cannot stop the soldiers. Many more live in their log walls and will come out to take our brothers away.' Another brave got to his feet, challenging Kee-To's words.

'Listen to me. I will ride from this place above the trail the white men will use to reach their Iron Horse. We will camp above it out of sight. Each day two of us

18

will watch the trail below until we see the soldiers moving our chiefs. Once they are put inside the Iron Horse, I will attack only that car they are held in by freeing it from the rest of the train. We will kill any soldiers holding them and ride away taking our brothers with us. This plan will work even better if the Iron Horse moves at night.'

Kee-To's words stunned his detractors to silence. He knew the power of his plan now made the council warriors think again about the real chance it would work. This time he did not wait for any more questions. He struck while he knew he had the advantage. When he asked what braves were willing to join him, every hand in the circle went up.

The thirteen Sioux warriors made their way through snowy mountains, setting up camp above and well back of the cavalry trail. Each day Kee-To sent two men riding back to the canyon edge, watching below until dark. They could build no fire, staying alert and still in the freezing cold air no matter the physical suffering they endured. Late in the afternoon of the third day two braves came riding back into camp at a breakneck pace, snow flying from their horses' hoofs before pulling to a stop.

'The soldiers are on the trail with our chiefs. They passed below us!' One scout leaped down from his horse.

'Are you certain our chiefs were with them?' Kee-To questioned.

'Yes. They have them on horses, roped together. Their hands are tied behind their backs.'

'Now we leave this camp.' Kee-To turned to the rest of his warriors. 'When they put them on the Iron Horse we will attack.'

CHAPTER TWO

Captain Stodlmeyer rode at the head of his line of troopers with their Sioux captives boxed in the middle. Big Hair rode at his side. Turning to his lead tracker, he offered a comment and question. 'I don't see any other tracks here, only the ones we're making. I'm glad to see we're alone without any interference, aren't you?'

For several moments Big Hair did not respond, still studying the blanket of snow as they rode ahead. When he did, his comment didn't support Stodlmeyer's quick conclusion.

'Snow only . . . two day old. Others could . . . ride this way . . . too.'

'Well, that's a pretty big maybe. All I want is to get these Sioux troublemakers on this train and off to Fort Riley without any more problems. That renegade Kee-To is still on the loose. He'll be next to take the same ride, once I get my hands on him again.'

'Maybe . . . maybe no. He is . . . Spirit Chief. No white man . . . can take him.'

'Don't tell me you believe a cock and bull story like

that. I thought by now you'd know better, living with us at the outpost. I see civilization hasn't rubbed off on you as I hoped it might.'

'You no . . . keep him . . . before.'

'That was because my bumbling guards did not do their job as they should have. Instead they were too busy trying to keep warm. There's nothing "mystical" about that.'

'Kee-To is. . . Spirit Warrior . . . he has big . . . medicine, like I tell you . . . but you no . . . listen.'

Stodlmeyer turned away in disgust. He wondered why he'd even tried to have a conversation with this half-breed in the first place. Big Hair might ride with the cavalry and sleep inside outpost walls, but his old Indian superstitions would not die away.

The captain left Sergeant Merchant in charge of the barracks in his absence and Lieutenant Steven Commer of the overall outpost. He personally wanted to put the Sioux chiefs on the train, even if it meant being gone for six days. He could not take the long trip south to Fort Riley, much as he'd wished he could. The briefcase containing all his notes and other information the army officers would need to successfully prosecute the case against the chiefs would be delivered by First Sergeant David McNerny.

When the line of blue coats rode out of the deep canyon onto rolling flats days later the low arc of winter sun was already being swallowed up by surrounding mountains and it was growing dark. But the outline of the engine and its two trailing cars was still visible. Stodlmeyer kicked his horse ahead at a faster pace, anxious to finally release his charges in a successful changeover. Of the twenty cavalrymen riding with him, ten would board the train to guard the five chiefs on their trip. The first sergeant would be in charge of them, too.

The sound of the belching engine grew louder as the riders came up and the captain eased down from the saddle, ordering McNerny to do the same and get the Indians up into the single passenger car. All five climbed the steel steps into the railcar, noticing the soft glow of kerosene lamps mounted on both walls. They were ordered to sit down in the middle of the car so guards could box them in both front and back.

'You keep these lamps lit all night,' Stodlmeyer ordered, standing at the head of the car. 'That's the only way you and your men can keep an eye on this bunch.'

'I will, sir. You can count on it,' McNerny assured him.

'And use your men in shifts, so half sleep while the others stay awake on guard.'

'Very good, sir. I certainly will.'

Three short, loud blasts on the engine whistle signaled that the engineer was ready to leave. Stodlmeyer eyed the Indians one last time before turning back to his first sergeant.

'All right, they're in your hands now. Remember what I said. Don't take your eyes off them for one moment day or night. And keep those cuffs and leg chains on them too. I've given you enough men to control any possible situation. You should have no problems if you stay on top of everything. I'll see you when you return. Be sure and give my compliments to Colonel Wellstone when you

23

reach the fort and be certain he gets all my notes in the briefcase.'

'I'll see to all of it, sir,' McNerny saluted as Stodlmeyer turned to exit the car and went down the steps.

After mounting, the captain rode up to the engine, hailing the engineer over the hiss and roar of the firebox. 'My people are on board along with the Indian captives,' he shouted. 'Get them out of here and on their way!'

The engineer waved a gloved hand as the big steel pistons began slowly pumping the wheels to the ring of steel on steel. A cloud of black smoke belched out of the stack and the train lurched forward. Stodlmeyer reined his nervous horse back at the sudden sound and a shower of golden sparks that spiraled up with the smoke looking like Fourth of July fireworks. A smile lit the captain's face. He'd done his job, and done it well. When the trial was over and all the Sioux hanged, positive remarks recorded on his military record could also mean another important rise in rank and more pay. The remaining troopers rode up alongside him, watching the train move away and grow smaller into the night, before turning their horses back across the flats heading into the shelter of timber and a night-time tent camp.

What Stodlmeyer could not know was that his nemesis was only three short miles away sitting on his horse along with his braves under thick pines, waiting on the rise the train must climb and which Kee-To knew it would be slow to top out. Kee-To had heard the three distant blasts of the engine whistle when the train readied to leave and knew it would come chugging into sight shortly. Turning to his braves, he went over his plan one final time to be certain they all knew their role and the timing to carry it out. Finishing, he asked if any questions still remained. No warrior spoke.

'It is good, my brothers. Soon our chiefs will ride with us.'

Farley Tents, the engineer, gripped the long steel throttle bar handle, firmly pushing it all the way forward while turning to his fireman. 'Delbert, we're about to start up the grade. I'll need all the strokes these old drivers' still got left in'm. Load that firebox right up back to the door!'

Farley leaned out the cab window, looking ahead into the icy glow of night-time timber. The bitter bite of winter air stung his face and made his eyes water even through his heavy beard. He wiped away tears with the back of his gloved hand as the steel drivers changed to a slower pitch, starting up. Ahead, Kee-To tensed, watching the roaring engine beginning to climb, coming closer. Warriors behind him held dancing horses in place as the noise grew in intensity and the ground began to shake under their feet until the big iron horse with its wood tender and railcar roared past with a quick glimpse of the chiefs in the lighted car. Kee-To instantly kicked his big gray and white dappled horse out from under trees and down onto the gravely berm, trying to catch up to the red-eyed lantern light on the rear of the car. For several moments more the train continued to pull away until he dug his heels harder into the horse's ribs and the powerful animal responded. Stride by stride, horse and rider began inching closer. Up ahead the engine laboured and slowed even more to the steepening grade. Now Kee-to reached the railcar. Leaning out, he grabbed its steel hand rail, pulling himself up onto the platform in one powerful leap. A quick look back showed the warriors closing in right behind him.

The Sioux chief edged around the platform, quickly climbing the ladder to the roof of the jostling, swaying car and making his way, at a crouch, along its top until he climbed down the ladder on the other end.

'Did you just hear something?' One trooper questioned a friend sitting next to him.

'Like what?' He glanced away from the chiefs he was watching.

'I'm not sure. I thought I heard something hitting against the car?' He pressed his face to the window, staring out into the black of night.

On the platform, Kee-To knelt, grabbing the lynchpin securing the car to the wood tender. Pulling up with all his might, it barely moved a fraction of an inch. He braced himself, taking in a deep breath. Reefing up on it again, it moved a bit more. Again and again he repeated the struggle until at last the pin came up free in his hands and the tender slowly began pulling away. On his feet again, he grabbed the round steel manual brake handle with both hands, turning it down. Icy steel brakes squealed and took hold as the car began to slow. He leaned far out, looking back to see his warriors waving. They were on board, too.

Inside the passenger car, First Sergeant McNerny suddenly realized they were slowing down as the sound of the engine faded away. He jumped to his feet, ready to sound an alarm, when Kee-To suddenly burst through the door, pistol in hand, and his braves stormed the other end of the car. The thunderous, one-sided gun battle that erupted lasted less than a minute. Totally surprised soldiers, half of them asleep, were caught off guard at nearly point-blank range. Four blue coats went down in the aisle wounded or dying at the first volley of shots as an acrid cloud of blue gun smoke rolled through the car. McNerny made the fifth, hit once in the side of his neck, a second bullet in his ribs. He slumped to the floor between the seats, his unfired pistol still clutched in his hand.

Kee-To ran down the aisle, straddling him. Leaning down, he tore the key ring loose from his belt loop. Their eyes met for only as instant. Later, after he'd recovered, McNerny would tell a military court of inquiry, in a horse whisper because of his wound, that he'd never seen that kind of dark hate in any man's eyes before or since.

Kee-To tossed the key ring to his braves, who quickly unlocked the handcuffs and leg irons on the chiefs. 'Get the blue coats' rifles and cartridge belts,' he shouted. 'Now we ride!'

Once outside, mounted double, the Sioux raiders kicked their horses away into the night as the sound of the engine backing down the tracks grew louder until it reached the railcar, coming to a steaming stop. Farley Tents ordered Delbert to stay in the cab while he climbed down the steps, running back to the still lit car. Wondering what in the world had happened, he cautiously pushed the door open and stepped inside. The

27

carnage and smell of death that met him made Tents stagger back, grabbing the back of a seat for support. 'Great God Almighty,' he barely got the words out, looking around. 'What in hell has happened in here!'

The warrior chief unrelentingly pushed his band of freed Sioux chiefs for the next two weeks, putting as much ground between them and the train massacre as possible. Kee-To knew all too well that once word got out of the bloody escape the army would send every available cavalryman in the territory after them in a bid for quick retribution. A humiliating defeat of this magnitude had to be reversed by quickly tracking down the band and hanging its leader in a public square for all to see, including the chiefs that would shortly follow him. Any trial, however short, would be an irritating and inconvenient waste of time. The name Kee-To Iron Hand hung on the lips of every trooper and officer like a dirty word that had to be spit out.

The daring Sioux leader also knew he faced an even more difficult task after taking the train. The chiefs, including him, had been summoned to Captain Stodlmeyer's outpost under the guise of peace talks. That meant Stodlmeyer knew the exact location of each village its chief had traveled from. Each was now also vulnerable to attack. Kee-To began to formulate a plan, as they rode, to try to convince the five chiefs when they returned to each village to immediately take down their teepees and prepare to move.

'If we do not,' he told the five one evening when they'd stopped to build a campfire and warm up, 'the horse soldiers will now ride into each one and attack us, including our women, children and old men.'

'But where would we go?' Running Horse raised the question. 'Winter is at hand, and my people want to stay warm in their teepees. To travel now would be too hard on everyone.'

'It will be even harder for the horse soldiers. They cannot move far with their extra horses, their many wagons and big wheel guns. We can leave them far behind if we move now.'

Buffalo Horn spoke up. 'You say we must take all our people and move. You did not answer Running Horse. Where would we move to?'

'I say we take all five tribes and ride west where the sun sleeps each day, farther into the mountains. The longer soldiers must ride from their log walls, the slower and fewer they will be. I have been in the country beyond the Blue Cloud Mountains. We would be safe there for a long time. When the sun warms the land again, we can move even further if we need to. The white men will give up looking for us after that. We are in our own land here. Our fathers and their fathers have lived here always. No white man can ever know it like we do. We will use that against them. It is as powerful as all our bows, arrows, spears and guns.'

Hawk's Eye had listened patiently without saying a word. Now he spoke up. 'Our tribes still live far apart from each other. To move as one, as you say, we would all have to come together. Where would that place be?'

'Here.' Kee-To leaned forward, beginning to draw a map in the snow with the point of his knife. 'Three Rivers meets at this place. They will be frozen hard. We can cross there to start up into higher mountains. If soldiers track us that far they cannot cross with their heavy wagons and wheel guns. They will sink and be killed. That is why we must move now and not wait. Our strength is in our numbers. Not scattered as we have been.'

The chiefs' faces reflected deep concern for such an unexpected, daring plan. Firelight playing across their dark features clearly mirrored that. Kee-To looked from man to man wondering if they understood the urgency of doing what he proposed. Running Horse finally took in a deep breath, ready to speak again.

'I think Kee-To talks the truth. We can no longer stand against the horse soldiers, tribe by tribe. Already, too many of our warriors have been killed. Their mothers weep in their lodges for their return. It will not be easy to do all you ask, but me and my people will do as you say and leave our winter camp.'

Buffalo Horn looked at his friend Running Horse, then back at Kee-To. He pulled at his chin in indecision for a moment before clearing his throat. 'This war against the white man has not gone well for us even though we asked the Spirits to guide us through our medicine men. Every passing of a new moon sees his numbers grow stronger while moving farther out into our land to fight us. If we can ride far enough away, as Kee-To says, maybe we can live in peace again. I will tell my people we must go, too.'

Kee-To turned to Silver Buckle and Many Sons. Both had sat listening without the slightest show of what they'd decide. Silver Buckle finally spoke first. 'I cannot take my people and go. My wife carries my new son in her stomach. A trip like that might kill her. She has already had much trouble. If you can wait until the baby is born then we will take down our teepees and follow you.'

'We must go now. If we wait the horse soldiers can follow and attack us. The reason for leaving would be lost,' Kee-To slowly shook his head.

'I will come when the sun warms the land again and a new child cries in my lodge. I cannot go now.'

Kee-To turned to Many Sons. The older chief was battle scarred. His broad, brown face lined with a deep gash showed he'd been badly wounded by a bullet that nearly took his life. His wide shoulders hunched forward as he stared around the circle of his brothers, gathering his thoughts. He had fought many battles against the horse soldiers and was a powerful warrior Kee-To needed on his side.

'I remember a time before white soldiers came into our land. It was a time of peace, hunting many buffalo, moving where we pleased to the call of Earth Spirits. There were few horse soldiers then. We could have sent our warriors down on them and easily won any battle. We did not. Some time we even helped these white men survive, when only their bones would have shown when the snow was gone. As the sun made its circle in the sky, they rode farther out into our land. They built log walls to live in. Their numbers grew. They shot down the buffalo until the great herds were no more and we had to eat rabbits and our dogs. I am tired. So are my people. I will make this one last move Kee-To says we must. If the

31

horse soldiers follow us again, I will not move. I will die fighting them some place over the Blue Cloud Mountains.'

Kee-To put a hand on Many Son's shoulder, whose words of truth had deeply touched every Sioux in the circle. 'Then it is agreed. We will take down our teepees and prepare for the long ride. We meet at Three Rivers in fifteen suns. Tell your people why we must go now. They will understand.'

The Command Office at Fort Riley had previously been informed that the Sioux chiefs were to be brought there by train for trial before they received stunning news that they had escaped in a daring raid on the train itself. The name of the bold Sioux leader who had planned the bloody attack kept coming back as Kee-To Iron Hand.

Colonel Milford Greenwood sat at his desk with an obvious look of dismay on a face that was framed by snow white hair and full beard. It made him look at least twenty years older than his fifty-six years. The junior officers around him saw his irritation even before he began speaking.

'By now I'll assume all of you have heard about the escape up north of the Sioux chiefs we were expecting here for trial. Our best information from survivors of the attack on the train is that this renegade's name is Kee-To Iron Hand. It seems from what little we know about him he's not only the chief of his tribe but a medicine man who leads all the tribes, too. I want to know if any of you have ever heard of him? If so, speak up.'

The officers looked at each other but no one volunteered a single word. Leaning forward in his chair, Greenwood reached for the cigar box on top of his desk and took out a thin black crook of tobacco. Lighting it, he leaned back and blew out a long stream of pungent gray smoke, contemplating his next words.

'I'm fully certain we'll shortly receive orders from Washington to take a large complement of men and move north into country this Sioux "messiah" calls his home and roams in with impunity. A successful attack like this can spread like wildfire, fomenting even more trouble than we already have up there with other tribes. I mean to put an end to it as quickly as possible, and hang this wild man before he can do something else.

'Captain Stodlmeyer has not been able to handle the situation. That is now clear to me. I will take over and do it for him. Once I receive the orders we'll move north by train as far as we can. Then we'll have to unload supplies, horses and men to ride the rest of the way to the outpost. Prepare yourself and your men for it, gentlemen. Because once we start moving, there'll be no stopping for any reason.'

CHAPTER THREE

Teepees were taken down, people packed heavy personal belongings and food items, travois were made using teepee poles and loaded to the limit. Some were pulled by teams of dogs, heavier ones by horses. Children too young to walk in snow were also bundled up and hoisted atop the pole drags. Women, old men and younger boys and girls were forced to walk. All the braves rode horses. Everyone was dressed in heavy winter clothes, some even blankets, against the bitter cold. The huge effort to so suddenly abandon their winter villages and trudge for days through freezing snow to meet at Three Rivers became known in Sioux history as the 'Winter Walk of Pain'.

Slowly, day by day, the tribes began converging on the waterways until all five hundred Sioux finally stopped on its frozen banks. Fires were quickly lit to thaw out frozen feet and hands. Sheltering lean-tos were built, while Kee-To and his chiefs rode up and down the river testing ice to see where it was safest to cross. After the bitter struggle to get here, their stay was all too brief. Just two days

34

later, Kee-To announced he'd found the crossing point where the major river was narrowest, before branching out into three fingers. That evening around a roaring campfire he explained the plan.

'Our people on foot must cross first. The travois will be next. Last will be the horses and braves. Be certain the children are with their mothers, for they will be scared. I will walk my horse across first to be sure I've chosen the right spot. Tomorrow, we will start.'

Running Horse, Buffalo Horn and Many Sons gathered their people on the river bank the next morning in line behind Kee-To's people, who would cross first. The Sioux leader began edging out onto the dangerous ice, his horse skidding and dancing behind him yard by precious yard until he reached mid-stream and the blue ice under the animal's feet. He did not stop or hesitate, even when the sound of cracking ice met his ears, and approached the far bank. Finally across, Kee-To mounted up and signaled his people with a wave of his arm to begin crossing.

It took the huge band of four tribes almost two full days to complete the icy passage with all their supplies, animals and people. Once on the other side, Kee-To only moved them another five miles before stopping to camp, build roaring fires and rest everyone. Steeper mountains now lay ahead. His people would need all their strength and will before beginning the long climb up into the Blue Cloud Mountains.

Ten days after the Sioux had abandoned their villages, Captain Stodlmeyer and twenty of his cavalrymen, along with Big Hair, cautiously approached the site of Running Horse's winter camp. At the edge of the timber, still over a mile away, the captain raised his binoculars and studied the snowy flats ahead. His eyes narrowed in disbelief. He lowered them, looking ahead to be sure of the location, then brought the glasses back up for another long look before finally lowering them and turning to Big Hair.

'Are you certain this is the right spot?' he questioned. 'Maybe it's over that next ridge?' he pointed off in another direction.

'Right place . . . they gone.'

'Gone, gone where? It's winter. No entire village is just going to pick up and move in snow like this. That's impossible. I want to ride down there and see for myself.'

After reaching the empty flats, Stodlmeyer reined his horse in a slow circle, as a new shower of snowflakes began spiraling down out of a dull gray sky. Leaning out in the saddle, he could easily read the many deep prints of horses, people and travois drags, all leading away in one direction. 'Where in God's name do they think they're going, and why now?' he turned to his tracker.

'Big Medicine, maybe move . . . them.'

'I'll show them big medicine, all right. I'm about to get the extra help I need to bring down every Sioux in this territory and now they run away like leaves scattered on the wind. Colonel Greenwood is due here in the next few weeks. What am I supposed to tell him, that the entire Sioux Nation just disappeared? Between now and the time he arrives with his men we are going to ride to all the other villages and find out what's going on. I can't just tell him I don't know what's going on. Let's get out of here. We've got a lot more riding to do!'

In the remaining days left, Stodlmeyer rode hard and fast, pushing his men near exhaustion, to reach the other four winter villages, only to find them abandoned, except for one. Silver Buckle's line of tall teepees were located in a hidden valley surrounded by thick pines, hung heavy with winter snow. Blue smoke curled up out of their poled tops as the cavalry rode in to barking dogs and, surprisingly, Silver Buckle himself, standing outside his teepee, as the captain reined to a stop. In the seconds it took for Stodlmeyer to dismount, Sioux braves armed with rifles and pistols came out of their buffalo hide homes, making the situation a dicey one that could erupt into a deadly gunfight at any moment. The captain tried to maintain an air of superiority, walking up to the chief.

'You know why I'm here, don't you? I want some answers. I want to know why all the other villages are empty, and don't tell me you don't know, because I damn well know you do.'

The stoic chief stared back at Stodlmeyer without answering. Seconds ticked away as the captain grew more irritated. He took another step even closer, trying to intimidate Silver Buckle, who stood wrapped with a blanket over his shoulders, dressed in heavy, buckskin pants and top. 'I . . . know . . . nothing,' the chief said finally.

'Don't give me that hogwash. The rest of the Sioux tribes cannot just pick up and vanish without planning something. I'll find them one way or the other, and when I do I'll have you and the rest of them hauled off to a reservation where we can keep an eye on all of you. I'm placing you under arrest, right now. You're coming back with me to my compound until I get some answers out of you!'

Silver Buckle didn't answer. Instead he suddenly turned to his braves and made one fast motion, drawing two fingers across his chest. Their reaction was instantaneous and deadly. All the warriors lifted rifles and pistols in a sudden thunderous barrage of gun fire, sending horses rearing and screaming, with several cavalrymen pitching head first out of the saddle dead or wounded. The chief reached under his blanket, coming up with a flashing knife and lunging at Stodlmeyer, who jumped back so fast he fell on his back while pulling his pistol firing as fast as he could. Silver Buckle staggered back, dropping the knife and falling into the snow. He tried crawling to his teepee but the life drained out of him, staining the snowy white dark red in blood.

'Retreat!' the captain shouted, stumbling to his feet and wildly waving an arm over his head before grabbing the reins of his horse and pulling himself up into the saddle. The remaining troopers followed him, kicking their horses away across the snowy flats while bullets whizzed around them.

Once they reached the protection of timber, Stodlmeyer ordered the remaining men to keep riding hard in case Silver Buckle's warriors mounted up and continued the attack. Even in the icy air, the sweat of fear streaked the captain's face as he kicked his horse ahead without let-up. He'd never come that close to being killed before and had never actually killed a man himself. Now he'd killed the chief of a Sioux tribe. He worried if he'd become a man marked for death with the rest of the Sioux Nation. He tried reconciling the killing, knowing now that without a leader the tribe would be nearly helpless. When Colonel Greenwood arrived they'd join forces to ride back and finish the job. Greenwood might also think more highly of him for the killing.

The train journey north from Fort Riley carrying Greenwood and his men was beset with irritating delays even before the engine could turn one steel wheel. Heavy rains turned roads into muddy quagmires, bogging down the heavily loaded wagons. That delay alone put the colonel's timetable back nearly a full week. Once men, horses and supplies were finally loaded on board the train began moving north, but rain turned to snow, loosening rocks and earth, which cascaded down steep banks and blocked the tracks. Soldiers had to get out and dig the rails clear before moving again. Colonel Greenwood cussed and fumed that all his carefully laid plans and timetables had vanished like leaves in an October gale.

After arriving at the mountain flat to unload, troopers still had several days' ride to reach Stodlmeyer's outpost. Greenwood had fought Indians before but not in country like this. Those battles took place near Fort Riley in relatively flat lands. This was all mountain country. And those tribes were the Kiowa, who had been resettled under an agreement with the government. But the Pawnee, the original tribes of that area, resented the Kiowa intrusion and fought with them. Indians fighting Indians was one thing. Up here in the northern mountains all that changed, and the onset of winter snows only added to his problems in facing the Sioux, who had long lived in this land and knew how to survive in it under the most brutal conditions.

When Greenwood and his troopers reached the outpost, Captain Stodlmeyer and his men came outside to greet them. The captain saluted smartly as the colonel stepped down out of the saddle.

'Hello Colonel. I'm glad to see you and your men made it through safely with all this bad weather.'

Greenwood gave a quick glance around the log-walled compound. Compared with Fort Riley, it looked bare and foreboding. 'Thank you, Captain. I've brought with me some medicine these Sioux you've been fighting haven't seen before.' He pointed to a pair of 12-pound wheeled cannons being pulled through the front gate. 'When they get a taste of that it will take the starch right out of them!'

Stodlmeyer looked at the heavy artillery, quickly realizing it would be nearly useless in steep mountain country and deep snows, but he held his lip. Disagreeing with a superior officer's conclusions was not the best way to advance in rank.

'Let me show you to your quarters, Colonel. Then we can settle your men, too. After that I'll explain where things stand about these troublemaking Sioux I've been dealing with and how I've already been successful at eliminating one of their chiefs.'

'That, I'd like to hear.'

After dinner Captain Stodlmeyer and the colonel retired to his office, where the orderly had a warming fire snapping in the stove. Greenwood sat across the desk from the captain, lighting one of his cigars, as he got comfortable. Stodlmeyer poured two small glasses of brandy, offering one to the colonel and pushing it across the desk, who nodded his thank you. 'Now, what about this chief, you mentioned?'

'Oh, yes. My men and I were out checking on the villages only to find them empty except for one. It was led by a chief named Silver Buckle. I went there only to try and learn why the other tribes had fled and where they might be going. Instead, he used it as a chance to ambush me and my men. When he wouldn't answer my questions, he suddenly lunged at me with a knife. I had to defend myself and shot him dead. That's when the rest of his braves opened fire on us, killing three of my men and wounding four others. We had to retreat fast because we were outgunned and in a vulnerable position, but at least I did get Silver Buckle. Without a leader we should be able to ride back and take the rest of them under control without too much trouble, except for some of the younger braves.'

'It goes without saying, I have to congratulate you on taking him down. That could be the key to any other engagements we find ourselves in. Once their leadership is taken out they lose cohesion. You say these other four tribes all left their winter camps and fled at the same time?'

'Yes, as unbelievable as it sounds, that's exactly what they did.'

'Have you ever experienced anything like that before?'

'No sir, I have not. And that's what makes all of this so

disturbing and dangerous. A mass movement of that many Sioux, instead of being scattered out in their own villages, means we cannot field as many men as they have warriors. We'd be outnumbered and outgunned, too.'

'Who or what could possibly cause them to move in mass like that and especially at this most unfavorable time of the year?'

'I don't have that answer about why now, but I can make a pretty good guess who planned all of it. His name would be Kee-To, Iron Hand. He's the same one who attacked the train I had the other chiefs put on to send down to you for trial. That's the kind of attack he would plan.'

'Yes, I've heard of him, but I don't know much more than that. If he's the chief who started all this he should become our first priority to lock in leg irons, or kill him in the field if we can run him down.'

'I understand what you're saying, but that's much easier said than done, if you don't mind me putting it that way, sir.'

'You were able to get all five chiefs in here once already weren't you?'

'Yes, I was. But I did so by telling them we could talk of peace. That's the only way I could convince them of something like that. It won't work twice, I can guarantee you of that. Iron Hand is the leader of all the tribes. They look up to him and his fighting spirit. He's also a powerful medicine man. To the Sioux, that's like a living God. They will go anywhere and do anything he tells them to. I'm pretty sure he's the one leading the other tribes.'

'Well, unless he can take all his people and fly like a

bird, he has to leave a trail a blind man can follow. Let's see how much magic he has to hide that. The sooner we equip our men to ride, the sooner we can go out after him.'

'What you say is true, sir. But he won't travel through country, even in this snow, where he does not have the advantage if he has to stand and fight. He is no fool. His warriors are equal to the best light cavalry we have when it comes to fighting a running battle in the saddle.'

'What has come over you, Captain? I believe you've been up here in this wilderness too long to think straight. He's one man against us, the United States Army, and every military advantage we have at our disposal. This Kee-To you speak so highly of is only one wild man made of skin and bone, just like any other man. He'll bleed just like that too, and die when I catch up to him and put a bullet in his chest. Remember what I've said. I mean to teach this savage a lesson he'll never forget for as long as he's alive to learn it, which won't be long once we move out and engage him!'

'I'm sure you will, Colonel,' Stodlmeyer nodded, even though he secretly didn't believe a single word of it.

Fourteen days later, far up in the deepening snows of the Blue Cloud Mountains, Kee-To relentlessly pushed his gray dappled horse higher, while the long line of Sioux behind him struggled to keep up. Already some of the old men had faltered and given up to the killing cold, dying alongside the trail. The women on foot took their babies from the open travois, wrapping them in heavy clothes and blankets and pulling them against their

43

bodies to keep them from freezing to death. The braves, seeing their desperate plight, pulled them up behind them and rode double. Through swirling snow flurries, all the Sioux looked ahead to Kee-To, wondering how much longer he would continue to climb before stopping to build warming fires to thaw out their frozen hands and feet.

As midday turned to late afternoon, the clouds thickened and blocked out any vestige of light from the weak winter sun, while five hundred Sioux struggled step by painful step higher towards the final ice-sheathed peaks at the top of the mountain range. Running Horse could finally take it no longer. He kicked his horse up the line until he was alongside Kee-To, leaning closer to be heard over the moaning wind.

'We must stop and build fires. Our people and horses can go no further. We must rest them and warm their bodies or many more will die.'

Iron Hand looked his old friend in the eye a moment before answering. Wind rippled the blanket wrapped across his chest and snow crusted his long black hair. 'We cannot stop. Once we come over the top and down out of this wind and snow then fires can be lit. Ride back and tell everyone we are near that top. We are only fighting ourselves to stop and give up. Every step we take makes it harder for the horse soldiers to follow us.'

Running Horse saw the grim determination in Kee-To's eyes. He knew nothing more he could say would change his mind. 'I will tell them but I am not certain if more will die.'

'They must not stop or more will die without the

sound of a single rifle shot. I hear the voices of our Spirit ancestors guiding me. They call me to keep moving to the top. I cannot turn away from their words.' He gave his old friend one last long look before kicking his horse away higher.

Somber shadows of early evening covered the frozen land before Kee-To finally crested the last icy barrier in a notch between the peaks. A quick look down the other side saw the mountains falling away into canyons and basins thick in snow-clad timber. But he did not ride down to the safety of their embrace. Instead, he stayed at the high crossover, wind driving icy darts in his face, while Running Horse, Buffalo Horn, Hawk's Eye and all their people came through before starting down. As darkness came over the Blue Cloud Mountains many fires were lit in timber pockets and hollows, while the survivors huddled close to their life-giving flames and babies were fed first. The brutal climb in savage weather had kept the bulk of Kee-To's warriors intact. If the white soldiers were foolish enough to follow them those braves formed a formidable force to stop them.

Iron Hand's journey into these mountains years earlier had shown large open meadows and flats even further down the mountains where his people could resettle themselves in a new life safe and far away from the prying eyes and rifles of the horse soldiers, or any other white intruders. That would be his next goal. In those lower lands where winter snows did not lay so deep, deer and elk roamed the forests and grasslands. The Sioux could live as they were meant to, hunting for meat to feed hungry mouths and prosper doing so. Spirit

45

Voices had led Kee-To here. He'd done what was ordered of him. In this new land he and his people would make a stronghold and the last stand of the mighty Sioux Nation. For now the ordeal of crossing over the Blue Cloud Mountains was over. Crackling fires roared high and meat was cooked in its life-giving flames, to feed hungry bellies and tired people.

It took Colonel Greenwood a full week after arriving at the outpost to get his men and supplies sorted out and ready to move. Captain Stodlmeyer had said Silver Buckle's people were leaderless with his death and they should be first and easiest to bring under military control. The colonel agreed with his assessment. When the full complement of cavalrymen rode out of the outpost, Stodlmeyer put Big Hair in front to lead them toward the village, while Greenwood eyed their strange-looking guide with serious misgivings.

'Is that the best you can come up with for a tracker?' the colonel leaned over in the saddle, talking in low tones to Stodlmeyer. 'He looks like he's half wild. Can he be trusted to take us where we want to go without leading us into an ambush?'

'I've used him for quite a while and he's never failed me. I don't see why he would do something like that now?'

'Well, he's part Sioux, isn't he?'

'Yes, I believe he is.'

'Then why would he be willing to lead us against his own people? That doesn't make any sense does it? Have you ever asked yourself that?'

'I don't know why, sir. Maybe he's had a falling out with them over some dispute. But he thinks like they do and does well tracking them when they don't want to be followed. He's better than any white scout I've ever had, even if he does seem a bit odd at times.'

The colonel straightened up in the saddle, still eyeing Big Hair, suspiciously. He wasn't nearly as convinced as his captain about their tracker's allegiance to anyone but himself. He'd bear close watching from this day forward, and Greenwood made a silent vow to himself to be certain he'd be the one to do so.

CHAPTER FOUR

The snowy march toward the Sioux village gave Colonel Greenwood and his men their first real taste of a mountain winter. It also quickly showed the problems in trying to pull their heavy 12-pound mortars. Thin steel-clad wheels constantly sank deep through snow into muddy slush, bogging down. The entire force had to halt and hook up double teams of horses to free the cannon before moving on again. Captain Stodlmeyer had addressed the fallacy of bringing heavy artillery along with them only once. When the colonel angrily cut off his remarks, he kept his mouth shut after that, while watching Greenwood's frustration every time they had to stop and pull the mortars out again.

At night the small field tents that the troopers set up had no stoves for heat. Only the cook tent and one other large one for the colonel and the captain did. The issue of one wool blanket per man meant all the cavalrymen slept miserably cold each night. That was repeated in icy saddles the following morning while being assaulted by snow flurries. It took nearly a full week to reach Silver

Buckle's village, where the soldiers arrived at midday. After signaling a halt, Greenwood lifted his binoculars along with Stodlmeyer, studying the long line of teepees a half mile away. Smoke slowly curled up through their tops along with a few people moving around them out in the open. Half a dozen cur dogs began barking and howling at the sudden smell of white men and horses on the wind. Binoculars only showed women and some children out in the open with no braves to challenge the horse soldiers.

Always cautious and ready to exercise precise military tactics, the colonel ordered the 12-pounders to be set up side-by-side for an artillery barrage before committing any troopers to ride in, while the captain studied the village a few moments longer before lowering his glasses.

'I only see a few horses and no men in there,' Stodlmeyer noted. 'We might not need the mortars to take the whole village without a fight.'

'Need mortars?' Greenwood turned to the captain with a look of surprise. 'Of course we need them. Why do you think I insisted we haul them all the way here instead of leaving them sitting and rusting back at the stockade?'

'I'm only suggesting we send Big Hair in to see if they want to submit peaceably. We might save lives of our own men doing so.'

'I didn't take that miserable train ride all the way up here from Fort Riley to bargain with a bunch of savages. I came here to show them any resistance is futile, if they can understand that much. A couple of salvoes should make it clear who is in charge,' he turned away from Stodlmeyer. 'Set up the mortars!' he ordered.

The cannon were loaded, the troopers waiting for his command. 'Set the range for 300 yards!' Greenwood instructed, the loaders elevating the barrels' angle to match.

'Ready to fire, sir!' the call came back.

'Fire!' the colonel shouted, wheel guns jumping in their tracks at the loud double 'Boom!' A cloud of blue smoke rolled out of both barrels, sending their projectiles arching high up in the air, coming down to explode in the middle of the line of teepees. Three shelters instantly shattered to shards, polls collapsing, shrapnel killing women and children inside, other villagers running from their buffalo hide homes trying to save themselves.

'Reload!' Greenwood shouted, pulling his cavalry sword from its ornate scabbard, holding it high over his head, as the cannoneers quickly followed orders, ready with a second volley. 'Fire!' he ordered.

The artillery shells exploded among running women and children, splattering the snow white ground with blotches of bloody red from the fallen victims. Those not hit tried crawling away. Before the smoke cleared from the second explosions, the colonel brought his sword down with a dramatic sweep of his arm, followed by one quick word.

'Charge!' he commanded, kicking his horse forward and followed by his men.

The cavalrymen thundered across open ground, snow flying from the hoofs of their horses, into the village with a scattering of their pistol shots and a few returning rifle shots from a handful of young boys old enough to hold a gun and pull the trigger. The struggle was brief and one sided, the vastly outnumbered and outgunned Sioux either killed or taken captive. Those left standing were rounded up and surrounded by the horse soldiers still in the saddle, as Greenwood and his captain slowly rode around the circle of cowering crying women and children.

'I hope you learned a lesson on how you handle these people.' The colonel twisted in the saddle, looking at Stodlmeyer. 'Now ask this tracker of yours why there are only women, children and old men in this village. Where are the men?'

The captain ordered Big Hair to put the question to anyone who could answer. The half-breed dismounted, walking up to several of the women wrapped with blankets over their heads, wide-eyed in fear, as he spoke to them in their own language. At first none of them would answer, until the tracker said something else neither Stodlmeyer nor Greenwood understood. Finally one of the younger teenage girls gave him a whispered answer, while shivering with fear and covering her face with both hands.

Big Hair turned back to the officers. 'She say . . . men leave . . . go find Kee-To . . . to fight.'

Captain Stodlmeyer turned, eyeing his superior officer. 'I thought something like this might happen. Maybe we should have ridden in here sooner and caught them before they could ride out.'

'We couldn't have,' Greenwood countered. 'My men weren't ready for it. Besides, when we find this Kee-To we'll just have more targets for our men to take down.

I'm not going to worry that much about their departure.'

'Well Colonel, I have to say any time Kee-To's name comes up, I naturally do consider it something to worry about. He'll be leading even more warriors now and that makes him that much more dangerous.'

'Will you stop idolizing this savage, Captain? With your attitude you'd be at a disadvantage even before we engage him. It's little wonder you haven't been able to bring him in up to now. Once I have him kicking at the end of a short rope, I'm going to send you on furlough back east so you can remember what it's like to be around civilized people for a change, and a change in your attitude, too. You need it badly to fulfill your role as a cavalry officer!'

Stodlmeyer held his response for several seconds longer, letting the slow burn of of anger subside. 'I can only say this, sir. You've never sat across a negotiating table and looked into the black eyes of Kee-To. I have. He looks like he sees right through you. He's not the simple-minded fool you think he is. He's cunning and crafty. He's also vowed never to be taken alive. I believe him. The more warriors he has with him, the longer our fight against him will last, and there's going to be more bloodshed than anyone can imagine. I fear a lot of it will be our own men, too.'

Greenwood looked in astonishment at his captain. He couldn't believe any cavalry office could come to such con-clusions about the Sioux, or any other native tribes. He even went so far as to wonder if this Sioux leader had put some sort of medicine man hex on Stodlmeyer. He had to snap him out of this state of mind, and do so quickly.

'If you wish to make this savage something more than just another man of blood and flesh, then help me get this messiah of yours into a simple pine box and bury him without a headboard. Once we do, I believe your mind will clear up and it better, or the only thing you'll be commanding is a desk in some office back east!'

The colonel had made no plans to transport the Sioux from Silver Buckle's village back to the outpost. That choice was not by accident. Instead, he brutally made all of them – women, children and old men – walk through snow and ice, sleeping at night out in the open around several large campfires, without the protection of tents or blankets. The results were obvious. Many of the old men perished in freezing temperatures and exhaustion. Half a dozen young children followed them in death. Greenwood ordered that the bodies be left where they fell, forcing those still on their feet, at gunpoint, to keep on moving. After the twelve-day march of death the remaining tribal members finally reached the outpost and were housed in tents situated in the middle of the compound, under military guard day and night. They were given no medical aid and only enough food to keep from starving. That condition assured the colonel there'd be no uprising by the survivors.

One week after their arrival they were forced to move again, still on foot, this time to the pick-up point with the train that would transport them over 200 miles south to desert country and their incarceration on a new reservation specifically being built to house the Sioux as far from their ancestral lands as possible, and the way of life they'd always led and known. This was the same government-approved policy that was being enforced on other tribes coming under the clenched fist of the federal government in faraway Washington, DC.

The victorious colonel thought only the icy eyes of winter had seen his unbridled enthusiasm for the brutal subjugation he'd endorsed and carried out. He was wrong. There were witnesses. Three Sioux braves who had gone out hunting for meat pulled their ponies to a halt hidden in pines above the village on their return. They watched as their people were forced to march away from the shattered village.

Yellow Robe turned to his brothers, talking in a low whisper. 'We cannot ride down to attack. There are too many horse soldiers and we would be killed.'

'I say we should!' Shining Knife countered angrily. 'They will kill the rest of our women and children if we do not.'

Yellow Robe looked to Spotted Horse. The older Sioux's eyes never left the carnage below. Finally he turned away. 'My woman and son are down there,' he nodded. 'No one wants to free them more than I do. Yellow Robes speaks the truth. We cannot change what has already happened. We are only three rifles against many white soldiers. I say the Spirits of our ancestors must protect them now. We must turn away and ride to find the trail of Kee-To, Iron Hand, and join him. He has many warriors who can fight to win our land back. Silver Buckle said Kee-To would ride for the Blue Cloud Mountains. That is where we must now go.'

The two warriors dressed in heavy winter clothing

looked at each other and back to Spotted Horse as his words sunk in. After a long silence, Yellow Robe spoke again.

'My brother speaks the truth. We will ride to find Iron Hand. Do not look any longer on our people below. We cannot help them. We ride for Three Rivers.'

The Sioux warriors pushed their horses hard and fast most of that week, through deepening snows until they reached the river frozen solid in thick ice. The original trail made by the passing of the four tribes was covered in snow, but the wide deep trench they'd plowed with people, horses and travois could not be missed. Following it up river, Yellow Robe pulled to a halt at the crossing point, studying the glare of winter sun on blue ice. Glancing at his two friends, he eased down off his pony.

'I will walk my horse across to be sure it's safe.' He stepped out on the slippery surface, testing the first few feet before venturing further. His pony skidded and danced as he led it carefully across to mid-river, and eventually the safety of the far shore. Spotted Horse and Shining Knife quickly followed until all three remounted and Yellow Robe took the lead, following the steep trail uphill away from the river. He wondered why Kee-To would take all his people on this perilous journey up into high mountains where deep snow and bitter temperatures would make it even harder for them to survive. As he rode higher the thought came to him that Iron Hand must have chosen this place at this time exactly because it would be nearly impossible for the horse soldiers to follow. A thin smile passed quickly across his face as he twisted in the saddle looking back at his two warrior brothers, steaming breath coming from their mouths and horses too as they struggled to keep up.

That first day of climbing began to reveal frozen corpses of old men who had fallen. They were covered in a blanket of new snow, looking like so many grotesque statues. He did not stop or comment on the grisly forms. He knew what had happened and that they could not be saved. All the Sioux someplace ahead had to keep moving or suffer the same fate. Yellow Robe kicked his horse higher, looking for the tops still far out of sight in swirling clouds of gray. Somewhere beyond that white-out world his warrior brothers had to be over the tops, leaving the stormy side of the mountains behind. He would not stop until he found them once again, to sit by warming fires and talk of the day when the Sioux Nation would rise up to take back their lands and the way of life they'd always known.

The endless 'clickity-clack' of steel wheels over rails droned on day after miserable day for nearly two weeks, while Silver Buckle's people and young wife were kept in open-topped cattle cars, guarded at each end by rifle-carrying soldiers. The only respite from the misery was that as the train moved farther south out of high country into lower flatlands the temperatures began to slowly rise, until the low arc of winter sun actually afforded a small degree of warmth to the icy chill. Outside the rocking rail cars, tall timber vanished to be replaced by lower thick cedar and juniper groves. Those too faded until thorny three-armed Joshua trees, desert creosote brush and cactus covered dry, barren desert lands. The Sioux peered over the sideboards of their rail cars at this strange new land foreign to them in every respect, until days later the squeal of train brakes began to bring the noisy train to a slow and black smoke stop.

Silver Buckle's young wife Winter Flower held their child to her breast, standing to look at the desolation surrounding all of them. No wagons were lined up to transport the Sioux, and no horses save the ones ridden by the cavalry officer and his men.

'Everybody up!' the officer shouted, signaling the Indians by raising his hands, before pointing down the steps leading off the cars. 'Let's move, you still have a two-mile walk to reach your reservation. Come on, every single one of you. I don't have all day to get you there!'

The long line of women carrying their babies, children and a few old men started down the dirt road. Half the horse soldiers rode along both sides, the other ten blue coats herding them from behind. Winter Flower walked in the lead, trying to look ahead until a row of long, wooden buildings came into view, surrounded by a tall pole fence. Closer still she saw half a dozen slab-sided cattle feeding head down in the brush. She would quickly learn those scrawny animals would be slaughtered, one by one, to feed her and her people until the meat ran out.

A large entry gate comprised tall timber posts framing both sides, with a third across the top holding a sign that pronounced, 'COMPOUND ONE, UNITED STATES GOVERNMENT RESERVATION'. Just inside that gate, a modest, white building, home to Mercer Hossel, the

Indian Agent appointed by the government to run the reservation and keep order, was the only other structure save the buildings housing the Sioux. Mercer was a tall, skinny man with dark eyes and a scraggy beard. His rumpled black pants and worn dirty coat matched. The short-brimmed hat on his head shielded his face in shade, so his eyes and features could not be easily seen. He took the black crook cigar from his mouth, eyeing the line of Indians coming closer. Flicking ashes off his smoke, he spoke without turning to another oddly dressed man at his side. His interpreter, Titto Luna, was a mixed breed Mexican and Apache Indian who could speak the dialect of several tribes including the northern Sioux. His clothes matched his ancestry; a floppy, wide-brimmed hat stuck with a single eagle feather in the sweat band, striped shirt and baggy pants under buckskin vest, ending in knee-high cowboy boots.

'So this is the great warrior Sioux I've been told were coming. Sad-looking bunch, aren't they?' Hossel appraised his new charges. 'Yesterday they were living like wild animals, free to run anyplace they wanted, and today they're herded in here like sheep. Maybe there could still be a troublemaker someplace among them.'

'No,' Luna slowly shook his head. 'I don't think so. At least not for a while. Maybe once they get tired of being locked up, or run out of that wormy beef you feed them, there might be. And look, they are almost all women. No young men to make trouble.'

'I hope you're right. I'd hate to have to send the cavalry in to punish them. I run a good, clean, quiet camp, and that's the way I mean to keep it. I don't want no government people coming in here snooping around, asking too many questions or telling me what I have to do. Once all of them are inside, you line them up and make it clear I'm the boss. Tell them if anyone does make trouble, they'll be put in confinement and not fed while they're there. Their days of riding around raising hell are over. You tell them this is now their home, and this is where they're going to stay!'

Inside the reservation gates, rough-built wooden barracks were furnished with only bare basics. The hard, slate board beds had thin, horse hair mattresses. No chairs or tables existed. All water had to be drawn from a single, common well in the center of the compound. Once every two weeks, one of the protesting cattle were pulled inside and shot by Luna. Gutting, skinning and portioning out the meat was done by Winter Flower, because of her position within the tribe. No medical help was available if someone became seriously ill. They either got well or died, buried in rocky ground in back of the compound outside the fence.

One seventy-year-old man named Stone Arrow had vowed from the first day of their incarceration to escape the desert compound and make his way back north to their native lands. He said he'd find Kee-To, to tell him what had happened, and where Silver Buckle's tribe was now held captive. Everyone ignored him as the ramblings of an old man trying to relive his days of glory fighting the white soldiers when he was a young warrior. However, when Luna did his usual head count several days later, he found the old man missing, immediately reporting it to Hossel.

'Gone, what do you mean he's gone?'

'l found where he dug his way out under the fence. He couldn't have gotten very far away though. He's the oldest one in here.'

Hossel quickly notified the young cavalry officer in charge, Lieutenant Miles Sutton, of the escape. 'Go get the damned old fool,' he intoned. 'He's seventy years old and you'll probably bring him back in two days. When you do, I'll make sure he doesn't try something like this again.'

The chase after Stone Arrow went on day after day for twelve long days without finding him. The scout leading the horse soldiers would find footprints then lose them when the old man headed for rocky ground. The lieutenant would have to order the time-consuming effort for his scout and men to circle out ahead until they could pick up the moccasin footprints again. On the morning of the twelfth day the riders came out of low hills to see the distant shine of steel rails, the very same ones that had brought the Sioux to the reservation. Sutton pulled to a halt, turning to his scout.

'What's keeping this old man on his feet? We should have run him down two weeks ago. I wonder if he even knows where he's going out here?'

'I don't think it's fear, sir. It's just the drive to get back home to his people. Old-timers like that place all their hope in being with their own kind. He won't give up the old ways, or old days, even if he dies trying.'

The riders started to move again, when the scout suddenly reined his horse to a halt, pointing ahead, shouting. 'Look, isn't that someone on the run, out there!'

Sutton stood in the stirrups, following his lead. 'By god, I think you're right. It has to be him. Let's go get him!'

A half mile away the tiny image of Stone Arrow could barely be seen lost in the brushy background. At that same moment a low line of black smoke began rising along the tracks, showing that the train was coming into sight heading north. The old man saw it too, quickly angling his run in that direction. That's when he heard the distant thunder of running horses coming behind him. Glancing quickly over his boney shoulder, he saw the cavalry riders bearing down on him. The old man ran faster, his lungs screaming for air, his heart pounding like a jackhammer in his chest. He had to reach that iron horse. He had to get on board and leave the horse soldiers fading away behind him.

Closing in on the tracks, the engine steamed past him, with the rail cars following one by one. His wobbly legs felt like they'd collapse any second as he put on a final burst of desperate speed when the caboose came up alongside him. His hand reached out for the rail bar above the steps. He felt the cold steel of it, pulling himself up onto the steps. At last he'd made it! Suddenly a volley of pistol shots rang out behind him. Bullets cut into his skinny body. He clung desperately to the rail only seconds longer before the life drained out of him and he lost his grip, falling to a rolling stop as the train, and his last chance for freedom, pulled farther and farther away.

Lieutenant Sutton rode up, yanking his horse to a stop. Getting down, pistol still in his hand, he walked up to the broken body as the scout followed, both men looking down without speaking at first, until the scout finally broke the silence.

'That was some chase, wasn't it?'

'Yes, it was,' Sutton's voice was low with disappointment. 'I'd much rather have taken him back alive than have it end like this, killing an old man. That's not what I joined the cavalry for, not even close. I take no pride in it.'

'The old man asked for it. He knew what he'd get trying to escape. It's no one's fault but his own. The only question now is do you want to leave him here or bury him some place around here?'

'No, we'll take his body back with us and let his own people take care of him. I read someplace an Indian's spirit will wander aimlessly forever if they don't enter the Spirit World properly, sent there by their own kind.'

'You really don't believe in that kind of thing, do you, lieutenant?'

Sutton stared back, thinking the question over. 'I didn't believe a seventy-year-old man could elude us for two weeks and then nearly make it to a train to escape either, but he did. Where did he get that kind of strength and endurance? We're taking him back to his people.' Sutton turned, pulling himself up in the saddle with one last order. 'You men get a blanket and some rope and get his body on a horse.'

CHAPTER FIVE

The successful and relatively easy campaign in taking Silver Buckle's village only buoyed Colonel Greenwood's confidence. He believed his field tactics and command were infallible and would carry over when facing Kee-To, Iron Hand. He was anxious to begin the march and final assault on the Sioux Nation and its vaunted leader.

After dinner back at the outpost, the colonel stood pacing back and forth at the end of the table in front of Captain Stodlmeyer and his own junior officers, cocksure of his plans to bring Kee-To to his knees.

'I tell you gentlemen, this Sioux they call Iron Hand will be crushed like putty in my hands once I catch up to him. He's gotten away with bloody murder up until now because he's never had to face a superior cavalry force. I'm going to teach this wild man a lesson he'll never forget about what the white man can do when motivated. When I'm done with him he'll wish he was never born Sioux or anything else. Captain Stodlmeyer has faced him over a negotiating table and seems to think he's a force to be reckoned with. His personal experience is worth listening to, so I'll invite him to stand and tell us what to expect when we engage this savage. You may be able to learn something beneficial from his remarks, or be left with more questions.'

Stodlmeyer was surprised at the colonel's sudden invitation. Both men knew about their disagreement over Kee-To's abilities, and what each thought he was capable of. Now he was being put at odds questioning a superior officer's assumptions. The captain had to walk a fine line in any remarks he made, yet the colonel had asked him to comment. He stood, taking in a deep breath before walking to the head of the table and turning to face the men.

'May I speak candidly, sir?' he asked.

'By all means, do so,' Greenwood nodded.

'Thank you. I'd have to start by saying my assessment of this Sioux chief comes from sitting across a table trying to negotiate a bargain with him for peace. He's not like any Indian I've ever met or dealt with before. He looks at us from a position of his victories in the field. My conclusions are therefore somewhat different from Colonel Greenwood's.'

'And what are they?' Greenwood raised his voice and interrupted the captain, hoping at the same time to embarrass him.

'Basically sir, he believes we are invaders in his ancestral lands and must be stopped at all costs. He sees only all-out war as the salvation of the Sioux Nation. He has told me, face to face, that his ancestors have lived here for all time and we are the interlopers. He also does not believe that any horse soldier can match one of his warrior's fighting

64

spirit, one on one, in the field of battle. In short, he thinks we are people inferior to his own. He will not sign any peace treaty that does not guarantee the removal of all whites, military and civilian, from these lands.'

'You had him and the other chiefs here under guard, didn't you?' Greenwood questioned again.

'Yes, I did.'

'And he escaped, did he not?'

'Yes, he eluded us by digging out of quarters where we had him guarded in the middle of the night.'

'And he also successfully attacked the train taking the remaining chiefs away to the reservation down south, didn't he, Captain?'

'He did carry out that attack and free them, yes.'

'Then I put the proposition to you that it's easy to see why you harbor such a high opinion of this savage. He's beaten you at least twice but he's never faced me and my men in the field. That is the real difference in this entire conversation, isn't it?'

'All I'm trying to point out is that Kee-To does not think or act like any other Indian or Sioux I've ever met. And that's what makes him so unpredictable and dangerous in battle. He may not have gone to West Point to study military tactics but he has a natural fighting ability to plan and carry out surprising attacks. Taking him lightly is asking for trouble. He may be far away right now but come spring he'll be on the move again. We cannot underestimate what he might do at that time. That's all I'm trying to point out here.'

'Thank you, Captain. I'm certain we've all gained some small measure of respect for this savage with your remarks. I'm going to make it a point to have you at my side when I hang him. I plan to move on him now, when he least expects it, winter or not. Prepare yourselves, gentlemen. Our campaign is about to begin!'

Captain Stodlmeyer's words were prophetic. On that very same evening, far away over the Blue Cloud Mountains separating the two forces, Kee-To stood in the pine-built lodge he and the other Sioux chiefs had erected to hold council in. A roaring fire at its center warmed the big room against the bitter cold of winter outside. When the circle of men sat, quieting down, he began to speak about why he'd called them here.

'Our people are now safe from the horse soldiers but that will change when the sun warms the land again and snow is gone. I say before that happens we must move again farther down these mountains into easier lands to defend. This also forces the soldiers to travel further trying to find us and bring their supply wagons with them. The farther away we are, the weaker they become. Distance is the friend of all Sioux. We must use it to our advantage.'

Buffalo Horn slowly stood from the circle of chiefs and warriors. He looked solemnly around at his brothers, before speaking. 'You say we must move again. My people suffered greatly getting to this place. Some even died. We are only now getting our fighting strength back. I say to move again only makes us weaker. Maybe the soldiers think the same way. Maybe they will stay in their village of tall walls until the snow melts away.'

Many Sons moved quickly to his feet, holding up his

hand to counter, while other Sioux began talking among themselves. 'Remember, my brothers, it was Kee-To's plan that we move all the tribes to this place at this time. It has been a good one. We have not been attacked. All the white soldiers are still far away over the mountains. Kee-To speaks with our Spirit Ancestors. They guide him to do right for all our people. I know it is hard to talk of moving again. But if Kee-To says we must, then me and all my people will do so.'

As was his usual habit, Running Horse sat quietly, listening to the different opinions and rising disagreement without interrupting. He saw the threat of divisiveness growing and knew he must try to end it quickly. Coming to his feet, everyone turned to him, oldest of the chiefs, and someone who always commanded their respect. Flashing flames played shadow and light across his craggy face and dark-set eyes. Many Sons saw his old friend take the floor. He sat back down. 'All of you, my brothers, know I have seen many winters come and go,' he began slowly. 'I was riding with my war horse, fighting the white soldiers, when some of you were still at your mother's side. But these years have shown me Kee-To has become the true leader of all our people. He talks with the ancients in the Spirit World, as Many Sons has said. His decisions are their decisions. I say all of us here must listen to what he says, and follow him. Silver Buckle did not, as Kee-To told him to. Look what has happened to him and his people. Just now three of his braves have ridden hard to find us here and tell us that a new soldier with white hair on his face leads the horse. He took all the people away, making them walk in the snow. Had

Silver Buckle listened to Kee-To, he would be here with his people and we would be stronger in number. I say do not doubt the words of Iron Hand, who has led us here. The white soldiers will only grow in number like wolves on summer meat. We cannot let our people become that meat.'

Running Horse's words silenced those that had disagreed. The chiefs looked around at each other, while Kee-To studied their faces. When no one spoke up again, he did.

'It is agreed. We will take down our teepees in three days. Each of you will tell your people to prepare for it. Tell them the farther down we move, the less snow we will go through.'

Buffalo Horn spoke up without standing this time. 'Do you know how many days we must travel to reach this land you speak of?'

'I say this many,' Kee-To held up the fingers on both hands. 'That place will be easier for all of us to live in and fight the horse soldiers . . . if they dare follow us.'

Once again the four tribes began packing, leaving the teepees up until last. The women worked steadily without complaint, while babies cried for attention, and some young men scowled at the work. Several teenage boys, still too young to wear the title of fully fledged warriors, argued openly among themselves and even their fathers that moving was an unnecessary mistake. But Kee-To had spoken and the Sioux had no choice but to obey and follow. On the morning of their departure, a long line of mounted braves, travois loaded high with bundles and some young children, plus pack dogs, started downhill leaving smoldering fire pits and trampled ground behind. The four tribes were on the move again, Iron Hand riding out front surrounded by a phalanx of rifle-carrying warriors, all bundled in heavy skin clothes, fur capes and brightly colored blankets. Only howling winds and new snow flurries looked down upon the long line of people fleeing once again to keep their hopes alive of living free, as they always had.

However, after traveling down the eastern slope of the Blue Cloud Mountains, a shocking surprise awaited Iron Hand and the rest of the Sioux following him. A four-man party of winter fur trappers had set up their base camp right at the edge of the snowline, close to the exact spot where Kee-To meant to re-establish the villages. Orlee Harp, Lonn Story, Gerard Manley and Jim Eye made up the group trapping this fertile new ground for lynx, martin, beaver and wolf. All the Canadians had come down across the border, working the area steadily south. Harp and Story had met Manley and Eye on the Missouri River the previous spring at the yearly trappers' rendezvous held there by fur trading companies to buy, barter or trade for the rich and valuable furs coming out of the northern Rocky Mountains. The four decided to throw in together and head south of the border working new ground, knowing it could be dangerous because it was well known to be Sioux country. They meant to trap right through fall and winter gathering as much fur as they could, before packing up and riding hard and fast back north for the border and safety. It was a big gamble, and they knew it. But the money that could be made was too tempting not to try.

The men set up their base camp working out in all directions. It consisted of a rough-built log cabin, the back half of which was dug out in the steep bank, giving it a cave-like appearance on entering. The front and sides were log-built, the back solid earth with a sod roof, and tin stove pipe sticking up through it for a smoke stack. Well insulated as it was, the cabin stayed toasty warm even through the worst winter weather by a fire kept going in a stone surround in the middle of the room. Tree limbs and branches were fashioned into bunk beds along both walls, covered in bearskin blankets. The four dressed much like the Sioux themselves, wearing full buckskin clothes and leggings topped off by fur caps. Now Kee-To and his band were bearing down on them, both groups believing they were the only human beings in hundreds of miles.

Kee-To used no advanced scouts as he moved down the mountain. He was certain the horse soldiers were far away behind him. When he finally pulled his horse to a halt nearly two weeks later, above the land he'd promised his people would be safe in, the hint of blue smoke curling slowly up through thick timber below sent a shockwave through him and his braves. He held up his hand, turning to Running Horse.

'Keep our people here while I ride down with my warriors. If it is trouble you'll hear shooting. Then come quickly. It cannot be horse soldiers, here.'

The older chief nodded, seeing the tendrils of smoke causing the alarm and concern. 'Be careful. You cannot know how many there might be,' he warned.

Two dozen braves started off, Kee-To in the lead,

urging their horses down the steep bank with the snow cascading in waves in front of them. All eyes strained to see through snow-laden pines, but could not. Reaching level ground, Iron Hand silently signaled half his men to circle right, while the remaining braves followed him left, to encircle the makers of the troubling smoke. The two parties joined in front of the cabin dugout, seeing four horses still saddled standing tied to a rough hitching rail. The smoke seen from above still twisted out of the tin stack on the sod roof, but no sound of any kind could be heard coming from inside the structure. The Sioux quietly eased down off their horses, following Kee-To up to the front door. His hand reached for the wooden handle, slowly twisting it up. He pushed the door the rest of the way open with a shove from the barrel of his rifle, his finger on the trigger ready to fire. The warriors next to him stood ready to unleash rifle fire hell, but instead the room that came into view was completely empty.

A low fire still smoldered under a large cooking pot hung on a steel rod-supported by metal forks. Four empty bunks lined the walls, unkempt, with fur blankets piled atop each one. A small board table with stump stools around it in the middle of the room held tin plates and cups, with half-eaten meat on a platter. Farther back, rows of thick furs hung from loops on ropes stretched from wall to wall, while dozens of other hides were still on stretching boards. Kee-To stepped inside. The strong odor of white men suddenly assaulted his nostrils, forcing him to stop and wince. The stink of it held him there a moment longer before moving further into the room, seeing supplies stacked against both walls. After a thorough look around, he spoke.

'These white men are trappers. They have been here for some time. At least they are not horse soldiers. Now we must find them quickly.'

Many Sons still stood at the door. His sharp eyes began searching the muddy ground. It only took him a moment to puzzle out the welter of tracks leading away.

'Four white men go there.' He pointed toward a small creek, still partly frozen over, a short distance away.

Iron Hand came back outside at his call, immediately ordering eight braves to stay there in case the trappers returned, and not to kill them but hold them until he came back. The rest of the Sioux followed him to the creek, with Many Sons in the lead.

'Two men go this way,' Many Sons pointed upstream. 'Other two go there,' he turned gesturing down the waterway.

Kee-To split forces, ordering Many Sons to take half the braves and start downstream while he took the remainder in the opposite direction.

Harp and Eye had gone nearly a mile up the creek checking on beaver snares they'd set the precious day after breaking through the ice to lower the wire snares on stout poles. The first set proved empty, but the second and third ones each held a large beaver. Harp pulled a rough sled behind him to haul traps and animals on. After rolling the beavers in snow to dry them off, he loaded them on the sled before starting back for their cabin, hoping Manley and Story would report more good luck, too. Coming through a thick stand of white-barked quaking aspen a short time later, Harp suddenly looked up to see Kee-To and his braves suddenly emerge from behind thick trees, their rifles already leveled on him and Story.

Harp dropped the sled rope, quickly raising his hands and talking over his shoulder.

'Get your hands up, Jim, and I mean real fast. Don't do anything stupid, either. They've got the drop on us and I'm not looking to lose my hair over it!'

Eye followed suit, letting his rifle drop into the snow, raising both hands, while Kee-To and his men advanced until he came face to face with Harp. For several tension-packed seconds both white men feared they'd be shot down where they stood as Iron Hand continued to appraise the pair without saying a word. If it wasn't for their hairy faces and white skin, both men were dressed almost exactly like Sioux. Kee-To finally spoke.

'You are in . . . Sioux land. Why you here?' He pushed his rifle barrel hard into Harp's stomach.

'We didn't mean to rile up anyone,' Harp was quick to answer, eyes wide. 'We're just taking fur. That's all. Then we mean to pull out back for Canada, if you'll let us. Honest chief, I swear on my mother's grave, it's the God's truth.'

'Can-ada?' Kee-to mouthed the word, vaguely aware of the big land somewhere to the north.

'That's right, that's where we're from. You know, across the border?'

'Did horse soldiers . . . send you here?'

'Horse soldiers? No, we don't know nothing about any soldiers. We don't want to run into them, either. We don't want no trouble from anyone.'

Kee-To and his braves marched the pair back to the cabin, hands tied behind their backs, where Many Sons was already waiting for them with Story and Manley under guard. The four trappers eyed each other nervously as they came together, wondering if they'd be killed at any second. Iron Hand ordered his men to guard the white men before walking Many Sons several yards away, turning his back on them so even his braves could not hear him speak.

'These white men say they come here from Can-ada. Do you know how far that is?'

Many Sons whispered he did not, but thought it must be a very long ride somewhere to the north. Kee-To looked away, his mind suddenly lost in thought he did not elaborate on. His friend stepped closer, getting his attention again.

'Do we kill these white men now? If we do not, they can tell others where we are. Maybe even the horse soldiers.'

The chief of all chiefs stared back hard, searching for his own answer. Conflicting thoughts played across his mind about these white men. He'd thought no one could ever find him and his people in this far away land, and yet he'd run right into four trappers, when he least expected it, right where he wanted the tribes to settle. Maybe he might be able to find a way these intruders' presence might help him for other purposes, rather than fresh scalps hanging from Sioux lodge poles.

'No, I will not kill them. They might be used for other things.'

'What other things?' the alarm in Many Sons voice was obvious. 'Our people have moved twice and suffered to get here to set up their teepees and build warming fires to feed their children. I say these white men can only bring trouble if they live. We should kill them now before they can tell anyone we are here.'

'I say we wait. Keep them in their log home under guard and away from our people. They have come here through lands we have never seen before. I want to learn that land and the trail that brought them here. I cannot do that if they are killed.'

Many Sons locked eyes with the powerful leader who talked to the ancient ones, the savior of all the Sioux people. He did not understand why Kee-To would not let him kill the trappers, but also knew not to question him further. He looked away with one final comment.

'I will have our braves watch these white devils, as you say. But I want to take all their weapons and furs for our own people. They can use the pelts for winter clothes and blankets. Winter will not leave these Blue Cloud Mountains for many moons. At least our people will be warm and safe while we wait.'

'That is good,' Kee-To put a hand on his friend's shoulder. 'In time you will see I am right to keep these white men alive.'

CHAPTER SIX

Colonel Greenwood, with Captain Stodlmeyer acting as his second in command, was now ready to begin his planned assault against the Sioux Nation in the Blue Cloud Mountains. He'd amassed an impressive force of almost one hundred heavily armed cavalrymen, two 12-pound mountain howitzers, two large supply wagons and two more Indian scouts working with Big Hair. His plan was simple enough: find Kee-To, Iron Hand and over-whelm him with superior firepower. On paper it all seemed to make perfect sense. Carrying it out in the middle of a northern winter, in mountain country, was to teach bitter lessons not found in military training manuals.

Captain Stodlmeyer had long since given up trying to explain any of the possible shortcomings of the plan. The colonel was in total command and wanted no further suggestions on how to change any part of it. When the large force of men, wagons and artillery rode out of the outpost gates the only thing Stodlmeyer could do was resign himself that whatever the outcome he would not be made responsible for it. Its success or failure rested squarely on the colonel's shoulders. It brought some small measure of relief.

Big Hair easily picked up the trail from the four villages leading toward Three Rivers. In the weeks spent following them more snow fell making the effort of such a large force of riders and their supply wagons slow and requiring great effort. A dozen troopers suffered frostbite from plummeting temperatures. They had to be sent back to the outpost, escorted by other cavalrymen, reducing the original number of men that rode out. By the time the remaining troopers reached Three Rivers moral was low and sinking faster. Colonel Greenwood and the captain reined to a halt on the banks of the ice-sheathed waterway, looking across to the other side, their faces burnt red from the constant bite of icy wind. Through a brief break in swirling clouds above, the colonel looked up at the frozen ramparts of the Blue Cloud Mountains. He said nothing at first, trying to conceal a long deep sigh by lifting his arm over his mouth, before turning to Stodlmeyer with a question.

'Is this chief scout of yours certain this is where the Sioux crossed?'

'Yes he is, sir. He says once we get across we'll find their trail on the other side.'

It seemed nearly impossible to Greenwood that anyone in their right mind would or could think of trying to take literally hundreds of Sioux on horses and on foot across the frozen river at this point or anyplace else. But the other scouts also insisted this was the crossing point.

'I'll have to see it to believe it.' The colonel remarked stubbornly, before ordering the cannons be brought up first to try and cross.

The pair of 12-pounders were wheeled to the river's edge, each one hauled by a single horse led by one trooper. 'Shouldn't we test the ice first, Colonel?' the captain suggested. 'There's a lot of weight in all that steel.'

Greenwood hesitated in thought. Stodlmeyer might actually be right about this one. He came up with a quick solution. 'Tell this scout of yours, Big Hair, to ride out and see if he can cross. If he can, I'm sure the cannons will make it, too.'

The scout heard the order but looked to the captain for confirmation. 'Go head,' Stodlmeyer urged. 'I think it will be all right if you're careful and go slow.'

Big Hair immediately got down from his horse, taking the first careful steps out onto the icy surface, leading the animal behind him. The horse began slipping and sliding on the slick surface, eyes already wide in fright, trying to keep its feet. The farther out the pair went, the more the animal struggled to stay upright until they finally reached the far shore, where the scout saddled back up.

'All right, it's safe,' the colonel's voice was loud and clear to the men behind him. 'Start the first cannon across. Let's get moving!'

The first steel wheel howitzer was brought up by one cavalryman on foot, leading the horse pulling it. Once on the ice the horse experienced the same skittishness Big Hair's animal had, but the colonel, on the bank, shouted for the man to keep going until he reached the other side. Part way across, the ice seemed to hold. But as the pair approached mid-stream, a sharp sound like a rifle shot rang out as the ice gave way underneath the hapless pair, swallowing up the trooper, horse and wheel cannon in a cloud of thrown-up ice shards. Shouts of horror rang out from the mounted troopers on the bank. For just an instant, the trooper bobbed back to the surface, screaming for help, grabbing at the slippery edge of the huge hole and trying to pull himself up before being sucked under by swift current and disappearing under the ice.

'My God, we've lost him!' Stodlmeyer's face twisted in revulsion.

'Even worse, we've lost one of our howitzers!' Greenwood roared, showing his complete contempt for the man's life as Stodlmeyer turned looking at him in disbelief. He knew he had to say something and say it now, regardless of whether the colonel liked it or not.

'You cannot take the chance on a second cannon crossing out there. It would be suicide and we might have a revolt on our hands from our own men. Don't think of ordering it, Colonel!'

Greenwood's face turned red with rage at Stodlmeyer's bold remarks and the tragic failure of his own plan. Those cannon were his ace in the hole and now he was down to only a single one. He was quick with another order.

'We'll move and find another place to cross!' He waved an arm upstream, turning his horse around, glaring at the troopers behind him. 'I'm not going to let this change my plans one iota. You men all hear me? We're crossing if it takes a week to find a way. Now follow me!'

Stodlmeyer quickly reined his horse up alongside the colonel as the line of riders started moving again. 'I'm telling you we're going to have trouble on our hands if someone else dies trying to get this cannon across to the other side. I'm begging you, Colonel, leave the cannon here. We can pick it up on our way back.'

Greenwood looked straight ahead, his jaw set grim with determination, before answering. 'When we find another place to cross, I'll have the howitzer taken down and across in pieces. We are going to use it come hell or high water when I catch up to Kee-To, Iron Hand. Do you understand me, Captain? That's a direct order. I will not repeat it, so you'd best remember every word of it!'

The line of cavalrymen grew stone cold silent as the colonel led them another mile upstream before finding a narrower spot to cross. He immediately ordered the last howitzer taken down, wheels, cradle and cannon in three parts.

'I want six men to slide the wheels and cradle across separately, with ropes, once they get on the other side. Then cushion the cannon by putting a tent under it. Get to work, Mr Stodlmeyer.'

'What about the supply wagons, colonel?' the captain questioned. 'There's a lot of weight in those, too. Ammunition, gunpowder, food.'

'Then have the men unload wagons and carry supplies across on their backs if need be. Once they've been emptied out, we can take them across with horses.'

'That's going to take a lot of valuable time, sir. We could be here for days.'

'Will you stop trying to undermine my orders, Mr Stodlmeyer. Just do what you're told. I'm tired of your negative comments about everything. Now get these men to work and don't let them stop until the job is finished, even if they have to work by firelight!'

The ice held at this new crossing point but Stodlmeyer's concerns about the time it could take came true. Two days and nights later the entire outfit was finally on the far shore, wagons reloaded, teams hitched up, the bulky cannon back on its wheels. Greenwood rode his men unmercifully every single hour of their forced labor, riding up and down the line of working, sweating troopers shouting orders and giving directions. The men were worked to the bone, worn out, until several in their tent that night whispered back and forth about actually deserting, taking their chances on the run.

'I didn't join this outfit to be worked like a dog because a mad man was leading it,' one trooper confided to the other three in the darkened tent.

'Yeah,' a second responded. 'You've seen these mountains up here? There isn't any way we can haul that damn cannon and wagons up there. I don't care how many horses we use. It's straight up. If he wants to get himself killed before we even find the Sioux he can go ahead and do it without me. I don't want to be any part of that.'

The third man had kept quiet listening to his buddies talk. Now he decided to have his say, too. 'These Indians are used to living and fighting in country and weather like this. Even if we did catch up to them none of us might come out of a fight alive. And I don't want to die without my hair on my head either.'

'Did Greenwood put a guard on the picket line of horses?' the last man in the tent finally whispered. 'Because if he did we'd have to get him out of the way, and I ain't for harming one of our own men to get at those horses.'

'We don't have to do that. Just tie up whoever's out there and get the hell out of here. We'd have a full night's head start if we move right now. What do you three say to it, go or stay?'

A long silence fell over the tent as each man struggled with his own fears. Minutes later the muffled rustle of clothes, boots, and jackets being pulled on was heard before the tent flap opened and four dark shadows disappeared out into the night, heading for the picket line behind the tents.

Hours later, Captain Stodlmeyer met another frigid dawn as he stepped outside his tent, pulling on his hat, heavy jacket and gloves. He started for the bugler's tent, when he looked toward the picket line and saw the night guard tied to a tree with a gag pushed in his mouth. Running fast, he reached the private, pulling his bandana out of his mouth and beginning to untie his hands.

'What's happened here? Who did this to you?' the captain shouted.

The young man gasped for air, trying to speak, while rubbing some feeling back into frozen hands.

'They . . . jumped me . . . sir. I thought it was . . . my

midnight relief.'

'They who? What are you talking about?'

'I couldn't see who, but . . . I think there were four of them. They were troopers. Then they walked the horses away before saddling up, so no one could hear them ride out. I can't feel nothin' in my hands. They're frozen stiff.'

'Get over to the cook tent and get some hot coffee in you. Warm your hands by the fire while I tell Greenwood what's happened here. Go on, get going.'

The colonel exploded out of his bed the instant Stodlmeyer began explaining about the desertion. Standing there in his rumpled, long underwear, his snow white hair and beard sticking wildly out in every direction, and without uniform, medals, boots and hat, the colonel looked like a small skinny little man of no consequence. He seemed almost a comical figure, but not for long when he began yelling orders.

'You get everyone up and take a quick roll call of what men are gone. Get me the names of these cowards, so I can write them down in my journal for a court martial when we get back to some semblance of civilization. Soon as you do, take a dozen men and go after them. Take Big Hair to track them down. At least he'll be good for something. Then bring them back here to me. I'm going to make examples out of them no one will ever forget, and I want you and them back here before dark. Now jump to it, captain!'

Stodlmeyer exited the tent without saying another word, remembering he'd cautioned the colonel about driving the men too far. Greenwood didn't listen. He never listened. The captain had long believed Greenwood was out of his element fighting in this kind of mountain country. Now he was certain of it.

Big Hair easily picked up deep tracks of the fleeing troopers, following them at as fast a pace as he could as the pursuers pushed the horses through the deep snow. Early that afternoon he reined to a halt, pointing far ahead to four dark dots on the snowy background.

'They caught,' he turned to the captain riding as his side. 'You shoot 'em?'

'No, we're not going to shoot anyone, least of all our own men. There's already been enough death in this outfit. I don't want to be a part of anymore of it.'

The four deserters twisted in their saddles, seeing their pursuers come into sight. 'Damn, they already caught up to us!' one said.

'We ain't going to outrun them, not now!' a second shouted.

'I'm not going back, no matter what. You boys do what you want. I'm still running on my own!' The third man kicked his horse out, heading for a canyon drop off a quarter mile away ringed in thick timber.

The cloudy gray of afternoon sky had just begun to darken and campfires had flickered to life at the cavalry camp when Captain Stodlmeyer rode in. Three deserters rode behind him, guarded by troopers, but the band was without Big Hair. Colonel Greenwood had paced a circle in the snow waiting for their return. Before the captain could even unsaddle he was already questioning him.

'I only see three of these yellow deserters. Where is Big Hair with the fourth?'

'He's still trying to run him down. The last one took off on his own when we closed in on them. I told him to stay on him until he has him. He'll bring him in.'

Greenwood walked up to the three with an ice-cold stare of disgust leveled on each one before he began berating them in front of the rest of the men gathered around the fire. 'So, you ran out on me like the yellow-bellied rats you all are. You won't be running anywhere from now on. I'm going to personally see to it all four of you end up in a military prison for desertion and dereliction of duty. But first, I'll deal with you here. Captain,' he turned to Stodlmeyer. 'I want this riff-raff handcuffed and in leg irons, to be certain they cannot try to run again. And I don't want them allowed to sleep in tents, either. They will be kept outside, with only one blanket, by a small fire just enough to keep them from freezing to death, under guard day and night. And put them on half rations too until I see them hung!'

Stodlmeyer stood dumbstruck. He couldn't believe any cavalry officer would ever give an order like that. His mind raced to say something, anything that might change the brutality of it. He took in a deep breath, praying what he had to say might work.

'Sir, how can I do all that once we start moving again?

'I've already thought of that, Captain. I cannot leave them here, or spare the men it would take to guard them, so they're coming with us. Only they'll be riding right up front, still handcuffed, next to our scouts, when we engage the Sioux. In other words, they'll be the first to face them in action.'

'But they'll have no weapons when any fight breaks out?'

'That's not my problem, it's theirs. They already showed yellow and should have thought of the consequences before they ran out on me and the rest of the men, including you, Captain.'

'But that's suicide, isn't it?'

'Call it what you will. I call it capital punishment for what they tried to do. If they survive, they will face a military court martial. If they do not, they'll pay for it at the hands of Kee-To, Iron Hand. Either way, justice will be served.'

The fourth deserter, Lucas Homby, was a Missouri farm boy raised up on horses and hunting in the outdoors before he came west and joined the cavalry on his twentieth birthday. His choice to keep running was a natural one. He'd pitted his skills and outdoor savvy against wild country many times in the past while growing up back home. He meant to use them again now against Big Hair and the winter mountains he found himself in. Lucas knew he'd be easily tracked by the snowy hoof prints his horse was leaving behind. Instead, he meant to use them against the tracker and kill him. He wasn't about to be dragged back in front of Colonel Greenwood and his insanity.

Homby had taken his horse plunging down the steep slope through timber so thick that when the scout reached the edge of the canyon he was already out of sight. Big Hair eagerly kicked his horse down after the lone trooper, certain he'd have him in a matter of minutes. The scout dug his moccasin boots deep into his horse's ribs, growing more impatient each minute he had to chase this last runaway soldier, instead of already being on his way back to camp. The farther down the canyon horse and rider plunged, without seeing the deserter, the more irritated he became. When he caught up to him, he'd already thought to kill him on the spot for all the time and trouble he was causing by running. He could always tell Greenwood he had no other choice. Just to make it even more convincing, he'd rope the dead body on his horse and bring it back to camp as proof.

Nearing the bottom of the timbered slope, the deep hoof prints were still easy to follow even at the wild run down. Up ahead Big Hair could see the bright white of open ground through trees. Once he reached it, the fleeing trooper would be easily overtaken and killed. Bursting out of timber, he yanked his horse to a sudden stop, scanning an expansive snowfield. The same instant he realized it was empty of any rider, a small movement at the edge of timber close on his right caught his eye, followed by the sudden 'Boom!' of a rifle shot. The white-hot pain of a bullet cut through his buckskin clothes, driving deep into his stomach, throwing Big Hair off his horse and down into the snow. In his last moments of consciousness, he became vaguely aware of the sound of footsteps coming closer through snow. Suddenly there was the dim shadow of a man standing over him, rifle in hand. After a moment the shadow moved away and the scout passed out from excruciating pain and loss of blood. The dying man never heard Lucas Homby mount up and ride away.

CHAPTER SEVEN

Cold darkness had already closed its black velvet hand around the Blue Cloud Mountains and the cavalry camp, but Colonel Greenwood still insisted he, Captain Stodlmeyer, the captured deserters, and the rest of the troops stay up around a roaring campfire, waiting until Big Hair finally rode in with the last deserter. The longer he waited, the more angry and abusive the colonel became, continually escalating the threat of what he was going to do to Homby once he got his hands on him.

The first hour passed into a second, while Greenwood stamped a circle around the fire, swearing retribution, until Stodlmeyer decided he had to do something to try to calm him and the situation down.

'Sir,' he began cautiously. 'Everyone here is dead on their feet and half frozen. Why not let them bed down for the night. I'll stay up and the moment Big Hair comes in, I'll wake you. There's nothing to be gained doing this to the rest of these men.'

'Nothing to be gained?' Greenwood exploded in pent-up rage. 'There's military discipline to be gained. Do I have to explain that to you of all people, a cavalry officer!'

'That's not what I meant, sir. What I mean to say is. . . .'

The sudden sound of slow hoof beats coming closer out of the dark, stopped the exchange, both officers and men turning to the growing image of a horse and rider appearing out of the gloom. Firelight illuminated the form of Big Hair bent face down, low over the saddle-horn, barely hanging on. Captain Stodlmeyer ran towards the horse as the scout lost his grip and fell to the ground, dead before he could utter a single word about what had happened. Colonel Greenwood ran up too as the captain rolled Big Hair over, seeing his blood-soaked buckskin clothes bathed in bright red. Stodlmeyer looked up at his superior officer. 'He was dead in the saddle but somehow he hung on long enough to make it back here.'

'Yes, it appears he did. And now Lucas Homby will be hunted down and charged with murdering a scout of the United States Army, on top of everything else. That's another thing I'll see to personally, if it's the last thing I ever do in this campaign!'

Big Hair was buried quickly the next morning under a pile of rocks behind camp, without ceremony or Bible. He would have asked for or understood neither. Captain Stodlmeyer oversaw the brief internment, while Colonel Greenwood ordered camp broken and wagons and horses hitched up, preparing to move out. The colonel abhorred failure in any form. As far as he was concerned, Big Hair failed to do his job and bring in Lucas Homby.

Why would he want to officiate over the scout's burial?

Greenwood still had two scouts left that had backed up Big Hair. One was an older white man named Loy Marvel, the second a much younger half-breed Indian named Quiet Eye. Marvel could speak some Sioux dialect that Quiet Eye understood. Accordingly, Marvel would do all the talking for both of them about decisions and tactics they thought best when conferring with Colonel Greenwood.

Marvel was thought to be in his mid-fifties or early sixties. He never said which one. Spry and slender with a wildly fuzzy salt and pepper beard that went completely around his face, he spoke in a high, squeaky voice, the product of nearly being killed by a knife slash across his throat in a battle with an Indian he was tracking. The Indian had killed a white man in a horse trade that went bad. Marvel killed his attacker with a pistol shot in the face, but nearly died from loss of blood before he was able to get back to medical help and stitched up in town. His thick beard covered up most of the ugly scar.

Quiet Eye was less than half Marvel's age but had all the natural instincts Indian scouts and trackers grew up with. If Marvel missed something on the trail, his younger partner would point it out. The odd pairing meant that together they generally did a good job for their once a month pay of forty dollars. Greenwood also preferred talking to the white scout instead of Big Hair, who had rarely given him a straight answer.

The colonel walked up to the pair as they saddled their horses, sliding rifles into scabbards. 'You two are now responsible for guiding us into these mountains. I don't have to tell you how dangerous this will be. I expect you to do your job and confer with me on anything you're uncertain of. This Sioux chief we're going after is supposed to be a master of ambush. Keep that in mind as we close in on him. Do I make myself clear?'

'Yeah, you do, Colonel. I heard about him, too,' Loy nodded. 'I ain't too worried about how smart he's suppose to be. Once "Ol' Betsy" here draws a bead on him, he'll die just like any other man.' He patted the stock of his rifle. 'There's no spirit a bullet can't stop. And that includes his, too.'

'Just be sure you two find him before he finds us. That's the key to defeating this savage once and for all.' Greenwood turned away, heading back to his troopers who were busy preparing to begin to saddle up and ride up into the Blue Cloud Mountains and whatever the days and weeks ahead held for all of them.

Once in the saddle himself, Colonel Greenwood proudly looked back at his long line of men, the wheeled howitzer and the two supply wagons. They were a considerable force by any measure, surely capable of engaging and finishing off the vaunted Sioux leader and all those that supported him. From the very first moment he'd received orders to take his men and move north to track down and finish off Kee-To, Iron Hand, he'd hungered for this moment. Now, at last, it was at hand. The feeling of pure euphoria was clearly mirrored on his lined face. He even managed a rare, small smile, while turning to Captain Stodlmeyer.

'I say the time has come for us to go find this killer and dispel any charade that he's somehow invincible.

Start the men, Mr. Stodlmeyer, and raise the company flag!'

The captain twisted in the saddle, lifting a hand high over his head, twirling it in a circular motion to signal the troopers to start forward. Somewhere far over the Blue Cloud Mountains, at least two long weeks of toil and misery away, the new Sioux villages lay, over one hundred teepees strong, filling the small valley they now considered a safe home. Reaching it would teach bitter lessons that began the very next day for Colonel Greenwood and his men.

Loy quickly pointed out to the colonel that the Sioux had started up into the mountains immediately after crossing Three Rivers, but Greenwood insisted they follow the river until they found an easier way up, such as a valley that led into high country. The scout countered if they did that either he or Quiet Eye would have to leave the main force of men and double back east through the mountains to pick up the original trail of the Sioux, then ride back trying to parallel it while still many miles away.

'That takes a whole lot of time and covering ground we don't need to do,' he argued.

'I say we stay to the river,' the colonel insisted. 'You two will do what you have to. I have nearly one hundred men I have to keep together and ready to fight. Don't waste my time bringing it up again.'

Marvel turned away with a quick shake of his head. He uttered low words under his breath that Greenwood didn't hear. Already he could see trying to explain things to the officer looked like it was going to be a struggle that could only lead to trouble that could become deadly serious as they closed in on the Sioux stronghold. His instincts would prove correct and carry with it the real danger of miscommunication.

For two more days the long line of men and equipment stayed with the river course without finding a notch into the high mountains where they could start up. On the morning of the third, Colonel Greenwood was forced to finally order his men to turn up into the mountains, taking them head on. In less than a hour, the howitzer and supply wagons were helplessly bogged down in deep snow on the rising slope. He, along with Captain Stodlmeyer, rode back down the line to assess the problem. The colonel was first to come up with a possible solution.

'We need to hitch more horses to these wagons and the 12-pounder. That should give us a bigger pull and break them free.'

'Maybe it would, but where are we going to get more horses? We don't have any to spare.'

'I've already thought of that, too. We'll use the horses the deserters are riding and have the troopers guarding them double up. This way we'll have another seven or eight animals. The deserters can walk.'

'Walk, in this snow? They'll likely freeze to death. Why don't we try instead to unload some of the supplies we can get along without and lighten the wagons?'

'I said they'll walk. Now carry out my orders and get them off their horses. I want those extra animals up here and fast.'

The three deserters were put afoot, still handcuffed,

their horses unsaddled and brought forward, hitched to the supply wagons. The cavalrymen guarding them looked at each other in dismay when Captain Stodlmeyer told them they had to ride double, giving up their horses, too. Getting down, one of the men turned to the captain.

'You can report me if you want sir, but these horses aren't going to last three days riding double up into these mountains.' he nodded uphill.

'I'm only carrying out orders, not asking for your opinions. The colonel wants to try this idea and that's what we're going to do. I'd suggest you keep your remarks to yourself, Private. Colonel Greenwood is not interested in hearing them, or mine either for that matter.'

The trooper turned away, knowingly glancing at his friends, clearly understanding Stodlmeyer's final remarks.

With the spare horses moved into their traces and hooked up, drivers began snapping reins down, shouting them forward, cracking short whips over their backs. Slowly, yard by precious yard, the wagons began moving again while Greenwood rode up and down the line shouting encouragement and orders. Captain Stodlmeyer stayed at the head of the line after kicking his horse farther uphill, then pulled to a stop to watch the long line of riders, wagons and the colonel's precious cannon moving uphill at a snail's pace. He knew more than anyone else they could never continue like this day after day before grinding to another halt. One quick glance over his shoulder at the high country waiting for them above made that crystal clear. How long would it take before the colonel understood it too, if ever, he worried?

That evening after dark, Colonel Greenwood had an aid summon Stodlmeyer to his tent. He crunched through the snow up to the soft glow of canvas lit from the coal oil lamp inside. Greenwood had just finished eating dinner and was sitting at a small fold-up table with a half-empty plate atop it.

'Sit down, Captain,' he gestured toward a stool opposite him. 'I want a progress report from you on our day's advance.'

The odd question caught Stodlmeyer off guard. He'd expected something else, not his opinion on the obvious misery the men had gone through. 'Do you want my honest assessment, sir?'

'Of course, I do. The double horse teams worked well, as I predicted they would, and you thought would not. That is a fact your personal opinion cannot deny.'

'Yes, we have moved a bit, but at what cost?'

'Cost, what are you talking about now? These men are being paid to do a job and follow orders. That's what I expect of them and you, too. No one said this was going to be easy.'

'I have followed your orders, sir. But when I say cost, I mean how long can men and animals keep up at this pace. We are horse soldiers and if our animals fail under us then we are little more than foot infantry, fighting the Sioux on fresh horses. If that ever happens, I fear they'll cut us down like ripe wheat under a scythe.'

'You must be delirious to believe something as pre-posterous as that!'

'Am I? Kee-To's victories have all come by him and his warriors being on horseback. And that includes his successful attack on the train freeing the other chiefs. We haven't even been able to see the tops of these mountains yet and it could take days or even weeks, before we do. Wearing out our saddle stock, pulling wagons and the howitzer, not to mention the men riding double and the rest of our troopers, only works against us. Time is on their side, not ours. I believe it's far more likely the Sioux will find us before we do them if we keep doing this.'

'Do you,' Greenwood leaned back on the stool, staring at Stodlmeyer. 'And if that actually were the case, how would you try to prevent it, while we're on this flight of fancy of yours?'

'I'd stop right here and set up a temporary camp to start with.'

'Go on,' the colonel mocked, a thin smile creasing his lips, folding his hands across his chest and crossing his legs. 'Then what, Captain?'

'Then I'd pick a small force of men, possibly six or seven, with Loy Marvel leading them, and ride fast for the top of these mountains and down the other side to locate the Sioux encampment. It's large. It should be easy to spot a long distance away without giving our men up. Once they do, they'd ride back here and we could plan how to attack Iron Hand and catch him off guard. And I'd do it without hauling these wagons and that cannon of yours around, too.'

'Are you done?' Greenwood raised his eyebrows, in question.

'Yes I am, sir. What I've said makes more sense to me

97

than struggling uphill like we're doing now, wearing out men and animals.'

'I'd have to say that's one of the most amazing tactical plans I've ever heard, and one based on the wildest speculation possible. Now here is my plan. Tomorrow morning we'll continue to double hitch the horses as we're doing now. And I want Loy Marvel brought to me early. I'm going to send him or Quiet Eye east to try and pick up the trail the Sioux made climbing up from the river. Then I can be certain we're paralleling it toward the top. Once we find their crossing point we can move down on them. That trail will lead us straight to them. And that's how we'll finish off Iron Hand and the rest he has with them, not some cock and bull idea about stopping as you suggest.'

'You asked for my opinion and I offered it, sir.'

'So you did. I had hoped for something that made more sense, but I'm not surprised at your overly cautious approach. You'll never move up in rank with that kind of thinking. Take my advice and change it.'

'Is that all, sir?' The captain made no further comment, knowing it would only be a waste of time.

'Yes it is. Remember to get Marvel here early. Good night, Captain.'

'Good night, sir.'

Stodlmeyer exited the tent and made the short walk back toward his own, thinking that Colonel Greenwood's mindless intransigence could only lead to a bloodbath if and when they finally met Kee-To, Iron Hand, and his warriors in battle. He was helpless to do anything except be swept along with it. Reaching his tent, he sat on a cot in the dark, staring at the snow-trammeled floor. Tomorrow was another day of misery. How many more would it take before all discipline finally broke down and the men simply gave up trying? He knew when that happened it would be just as dangerous to them all as a Sioux war axe or bullet in the back of the head.

The following morning more clouds with veiled bellies promising more snow lay not far above the cavalry camp as Loy Marvel made his way over to Colonel Greenwood's tent before being called inside.

'You called for me, Colonel?' he asked.

'Yes, I did. I want you to send Quiet Eye east of here to pick up the trail the Sioux made after crossing the river. You'll stay here with us. Can he handle that on his own?'

'Well yeah, I figure he can. But what good do ya think that will do to send him away?'

'I want to be certain we're paralleling them as we move up.'

'Why don't we jus' keep climbing until we top out, then work back down the ridge until we pick up where they crossed over?'

'Because I want to know how far apart we are right now, not when we reach the top of these damn mountains. In other words, I don't want any surprises. Do I make myself clear, Mr Marvel?'

'Yup, you do. If you want to waste time like that, I reckon you can.'

'I do not consider it wasting time. And you can tell the half-breed I want him back here as soon as he has an answer for me.'

'I'll tell him. Is that all, Colonel?'

'l might have one more question for you.'

'What's that?'

'Have you been in this country before?'

'I've been close to it, but not exactly where we are right now.'

'Then do you have any idea how much longer we have before reaching the top?'

Marvel scratched at his scraggy beard, squinty eyeing the colonel a moment. 'Well, at the rate we're crawlin' up here each day . . . I'd say maybe another two weeks.'

'Two weeks? Are you certain of that?'

'Yeah, pretty sure. I mean look'it how far we're movin' each day. Barely a mile, and it gets steeper on up. These poor soldier boys of yours are already plum tuckered out. This ain't no country for wagon and cannons. You leave them here, we'll make better time getting to the top.'

Greenwood eyed his scout suspiciously. 'Have you been talking to Captain Stodlmeyer about any of this?'

'Nope. Not when I wasn't talking to both of you. Why you askin'?'

'Forget about it,' the colonel brushed off the question with a wave of his hand. 'Get your partner started, like I said. He leaves today as soon as he can.'

Marvel passed the colonel's orders on to the young scout minutes later. The look on his dark face made it clear he wondered why he'd been ordered to make such a dangerous trip and alone. Jud saw that question, too.

'Listen to me, kid. When you find their trail, keep your eyes open. Them Sioux might be smart enough to have someone watching their back trail. You be real careful about it. Know what I mean? Now get to it and get yourself back here in one piece. And be sure to take enough jerky and salt, too.'

CHAPTER EIGHT

Kee-To's valley encampment had been well established by the huge gathering of the four tribes, who were finally able to stop running. Lighter snows at this lower elevation made life easier on everyone. Elk and deer meat hung heavily from poll racks cooling in the chilly air. And yet the question still troubled the Sioux leader about what to do with his four captured Canadian fur trappers. Several of the Sioux leaders wanted them killed immediately. Kee-To steadfastly resisted their demands. Instead he kept them under constant guard, using them as labor to do heavy work, their ankles bound together by a short length of rawhide thongs that made it impossible for them to try to run. The four gathered firewood, hauled game meat and brought in water when the women called for it.

Kee-To realized he could not just turn the four loose. They could easily tell the authorities or, worse, the military the location of the new, secret campsite. In the back of his mind he thought the day might come when he had to move his people again, fighting the horse soldiers and their growing number of cavalrymen in a battle he could not win. These four white men knew the way north across the border to Canada. That was their real value to Iron Hand and might be the only way left for him to save his people. Pulled by the demands of his chiefs and his own decision to keep them alive, he finally came to a decision, calling for the four men to be brought before him at a council gathering.

The evening meeting began with a big campfire roaring to life as the chiefs sat in a circle around rising flames, and the trappers shuffled in, under guard, still leg bound. Harp, Story, Manley and Eye stood, their faces shadowed in fear that this would be their last day alive. Kee-To walked up to the four, looking each one in the eye one at a time. Harp swallowed hard, ready to plead for mercy, even before Iron Hand could speak. Kee-To stopped him with a raised hand, and began to talk.

'I now know . . . what I will do with you,' he began, as the men held their collective breaths. 'Two will go . . . two will stay. If the two who ride away tell where my people are, the other two . . . will die.'

The trappers all breathed an audible sigh of relief, before Harp spoke up. 'But what two will go, and who stays?'

'That is . . . for you to say. Do so quickly . . . before I change my mind and give you to my chiefs.'

The men looked at each other suddenly, wild eyed with the realization two of them would be set free at last. They huddled quickly, talking fast, as the council chiefs and Kee-To waited for their decision without uttering a word. Harp finally pushed his pals back in line with their answer.

'Me and Eye have women and children back home. We've all agreed we'll go. But when will Manley and Story get to leave? You don't mean to keep them here forever do you?'

'They stay until I . . . say so.'

'You don't know when?'

'I will know . . . when that time comes.'

At dawn the next morning the pair saddled up, bidding goodbye to their friends, promising not to tell anyone of the Siouxs' location. As they rode off, Story and Manley looked at each other, both wondering if they'd ever get the chance to leave, too. The Sioux guards quickly prodded them away back to another day of labor, without either one speaking a word of what they were thinking.

With Harp and Eye gone, and the disagreements the four had caused between Kee-To and his chiefs ended, life seemed free of trouble and worry from the endless pursuit of the horse soldiers. The new Sioux camp was far from any white men and known to none of them except the trappers now kicking their horses north for the border, with the lives of their friends in their hands. Kee-To tried to relax and enjoy the respite from constant worry, yet he could not. Always his mind conjured up unforeseen events that could cause great harm to his people. He decided one evening to try to reach the Spirit World for their answers on how safe the Sioux really were. He prepared for it in his usual way, sitting alone in his teepee, stripped to only a loin cloth. A smoldering fire in the stone-lined pit almost burned down until twisting wisps of blue smoke rose toward the ceiling hole.

Kee-To leaned forward slowly, dropping small tufts of dried herbs onto the glowing coals, which briefly sparked to life, causing white puffs of smoke to appear. Staring deeper into them, he began to see veiled faces of great warrior chiefs of past years who had fought the horse soldiers in epic battles. One grew closer, his black eyes staring hard into him. His voice began as a distant whisper of warning.

'*Do not rest . . . the white soldiers are still . . . looking for you.*'

'Are they near?' he asked.

'*No, but they come closer, from over the mountains . . . you must know where they are. Do so . . . quickly.*'

'How many are they, can you tell me?'

'*That you must learn. Heed this warning, Kee-To . . . do not wait to act.*'

The face and voice began to fade back into twisting smoke. Kee-To raised his voice, imploring the image to stay longer and tell more. But as suddenly as it appeared, it vanished until only pulsing coals were left. Kee-To let out a long, slow breath of relief, bowing his head and closing his eyes. These intense sessions always seemed to drain him physically. It took several minutes before he opened them again, staring at the shadows dancing across the skin walls surrounding him. The Spirit Chiefs had spoken their warning. Now he must act on it quickly.

The following morning, he made his way to Running Horse's teepee. Smoke curled up from its top. Muted voices inside meant the trusted chief was awake along with his family.

'My brother,' Kee-To, called out. 'Can you meet with me?'

Moments later the older Sioux pushed the entry flap aside, stepping out. 'You come early.'

'I do, but for good reason. I want you to take five warriors and ride for the top of the mountains where we crossed over before coming here.'

'Why so far? That would take several days to reach.'

'I know. But I am troubled the horse soldiers may be somewhere close over the other side. Spirit Chiefs warned me of it last night.'

Deep concern instantly clouded Running Horse's face. 'You talked with them again?'

'Yes. I saw many faces. One told me of this trouble. I must know how close that trouble is and how many white soldiers there are. Our people believe we are safe here and so did I, for a long time to come. Now I can see that is not so. Take your men and go quickly.'

Running Horse nodded just once before locking arms with Kee-To. He turned back into his teepee and pulled on heavy skin clothes and a bear fur cape. Less than an hour later, Kee-To stood outside his teepee, hand high in salute, as the old chief and his chosen warriors kicked their horses away uphill until they were lost in the thick pines. He worried what his old friend would find at the top of the Blue Cloud Mountains. The Spirits never lied. That could only mean trouble awaited them.

Quiet Eyes' search for the Sioux trail had turned into a long, difficult ride fighting his way through deep snow up and down endless canyons that had horse and rider physically worn out. Marvel had thought he might make it in three days. Already it had stretched into four, with no sign he was even close. Each evening when he reined to a stop, he'd build a spluttering fire before curling up under a fur skin robe, chewing a few bits of jerky and salt, while his horse was forced to subsist on bare willow branches. By late on the afternoon of the fifth, he'd seriously considered turning back for the cavalry camp and take the tongue-lashing he knew Colonel Greenwood would deliver for his failure to carry out orders. Then fate played its inevitable hand, changing everything in an instant.

He was looking for a place to camp when he saw the only living thing he'd seen in a week of misery. A large white snowshoe rabbit ran out ahead of him from under a pile of snow-laden bushes. Instantly he kicked the horse ahead, pulling his pistol, firing three quick shots until finally tumbling the big hare ahead of him. At last he had meat, real food and enough to carry on another few days! But the desperate scout had something else too he couldn't know about. He had just alerted unwanted company only one ridge line away of his presence.

Running Horse and his braves pulled to a sudden stop, the old chief holding up his hand at the sound of pistol fire echoing away. Urging his horse ahead to the high point separating the two slopes, he unsaddled quickly and motioned his men to follow him. All five crept up to the high point, peeking cautiously over the other side. Barely one hundred yards away they saw the dark figure of an Indian kneeling in the snow, gutting a rabbit. The chief motioned his braves back down away from the edge. He'd expected to find blue coat soldiers and a vicious gun battle to take place. Instead he'd discovered a lone Indian. Who was he, and what was he doing up here in the middle of winter? For a brief instant he considered ordering his braves to use their rifles and kill the intruder where he knelt. But those nagging questions made him reconsider. A dead man, Indian or white, could not answer them. Kee-To would want those answers, too. He motioned his men to follow him back down the ridge to listen to a new plan.

When darkness enveloped the snowy mountains and an icy wind whistled up its shadowed slopes, Quiet Eye huddled next to a snapping fire roasting his precious rabbit. He lifted a smoking hot morsel of meat to his lips, looking up for the first time to see the sudden images of five Sioux warriors rushing at him only yards away. He flung the meat away, stabbing for the pistol in his belt, but not fast enough. Running Horse was already swinging his heavy steel rifle barrel down, crashing it across the side of the scout's head in a stunning blow that sent him sprawling unconscious atop the small fire. One brave quickly pulled him out, his buckskin clothes burnt and smoking. Rolling him over, he tied his hands behind him with a rawhide thong.

Quiet Eye woke, dried blood caked on the side of his face, minutes later. The five Sioux were sitting opposite him staring back, eating his rabbit. Running Horse got to his feet, drawing a long razor-sharp knife. Bending down closer, he put the cold blade hard against the scout's throat, pulling his head back by his long, black hair.

'You speak Sioux?' he whispered.

Quiet Eye stared up at him, trying to answer, but could not because of the way he was being held.

'I ask you one question. You don't answer, I kill you where you sit.'

The scout strained to clear his throat. Finally he got three chocked up words out. 'I . . . speak . . . some.'

'Who send you here?' The knife pressed into his throat with more pressure, ready for one quick slice across the jugular vein.

'Horse soldiers . . . send me.' He gave up the answer to save himself from certain death.

'Where are they, how far away?' the chief's voice grew more demanding.

'Five days' ride . . . west.'

'How many soldiers are there?'

'I don't count them . . . but many in a long line.'

Running Horse straightened up, glaring down on his new prisoner before looking back at his men. He said nothing but each of them knew what was coming. A major battle against the white soldiers would surely follow. The chief had one last order for his new captive.

'You will come back with me to my village. Kee-To will want to hear your words, too.'

Running Horse did not wait to start down out of the mountains with his precious captive. The vital news he had for Iron Hand could not linger until dawn. He immediately had Quiet Eye boosted atop his horse, led by one of the braves, and they started down at a break-neck speed. Horses and riders plunged recklessly through deep snow, dangerously slipping and sliding, fighting to keep their feet, hour after hour. When gray dawn lit the clouded slopes again the chief finally pulled to a stop, giving their animals just enough time to catch their breath while the warriors wolfed down a stick of hard jerky. After a brief rest they were off again, kicking the horses down on another heart-pounding run.

Every day since the chief's departure Kee-To had worried and wondered how far the band of Sioux had ridden and what they might find. After five days he spent time each day outside, gazing up the whitened slopes, hoping to see the dark line of riders coming down that meant Running Horse had returned with the answers he so urgently needed.

Another four days would come and go before, near sundown, that distant image of horses and riders finally came into view, winding their way down through timber. Kee-To walked quickly out from the long line of teepees to meet his trusted friend. As the Sioux rode closer he counted a sixth rider, his eyes narrowing, wondering who Running Horse had brought back with him. When the band pulled to a halt he stepped forward as the chief quickly got down and walked to Quiet Eye, yanking him down off his horse.

'I have brought you something better than where the white soldiers are,' he shoved the petrified young scout up to Kee-To. 'This is one of their scouts. His mouth will tell you all the answers you want to know, or I'll cut out his tongue.'

Iron Hand studied the Indian for a moment before speaking a word. He quickly noticed the empty black leather gun-belt he was wearing and the yellow bandana around his neck, all army issue.

'Does he speak Sioux?' Kee-To asked, never taking his eyes off the young man.

'Enough to understand and answer what you ask.'

'What tribe are you from? I can see you are not Sioux.' Kee-To stepped closer, nearly nose to nose.

'I am . . . from the Pawnee . . . people.'

'Are the Pawnee so weak you would ride with horse soldiers against your own people? Is that what the Pawnee teach their young men, to help the enemy of all Indians?'

Quiet Eye did not answer, although he clearly understood the question and its obvious insult. Instead, he shrugged slowly, dropping his head, wondering what was going to happen to him next. Kee-To already had that answer. He would take this scout before his council of chiefs that very night to ring every answer out of him as he stood, hands tied behind his back, flanked by two Sioux warriors ready to prod the truth out of him with short spears.

At dark the fire pit sparked to life, sending burning embers into the night sky, as all the chiefs sat wrapped in heavy clothes and colorful blankets. Kee-To led the first questions about where the horse soldiers were, how long it would take to reach them, and how many they were. In turn other tribal chiefs posed their questions while Quiet Eye answered each one as best he could. Before the roaring fire turned to coals, all the Sioux would learn the cavalry plan of attack, how they had struggled trying to haul supply wagons and their lone cannon uphill, and even the name of the white-haired colonel who led them.

After the scout was led away, Iron Hand began explaining his plan to engage the cavalrymen and defeat them before they were ever able to top out over the Blue Cloud Mountains. He ordered every battle-hardened warrior, and even all the teenage young men old enough to ride and shoot a rifle or pistol, to prepare to leave in the next three days.

The Sioux camp became a whirl of activity and excitement by day and well into the night. Supplies were gathered, horses fed well, heavy winter clothes pulled on, rifles and pistols loaded and all extra cartridges packed in skin belt bags. The air was filled with bold talk of the coming battle and its importance on total victory. Kee-To personally went to many of the teepees inspecting preparations and talking to his braves and their sons who would join them. He made it clear the ride to reach the invading soldiers would take at least eight to ten days, and that they would have moved somewhat higher since Quiet Eye last saw them.

Just after dawn on the third morning, one hundred fully armed warriors swung atop their horses to shouts and cries of victory, raising rifles over their heads. Women, young children and old men stood back in awe watching the huge gathering. Kee-To reined his horse around in a circle, calling out to his men that they were about to embark on the battle of their lives and one they must win at all costs. But one rider out of that hundred was not Sioux. Quiet Eye rode up front close to Iron Hand, closely guarded by two warriors flanking him. If he made one false move to break away they had orders to kill him quickly. If he wanted to live at least a little longer

112

he would show the way back to the cavalry camp. Quiet Eye had chosen life.

Even Lonn Story and Gerard Manley were allowed to watch, guarded by several Sioux braves.

'Would you look at that,' Manley exclaimed, slowly shaking his head in amazement. 'It must mean they're leaving for a major battle of some kind.'

'Yeah, it does,' Story answered. 'I'd give anything to have a horse under me, leaving this place as far behind as possible. What if Kee-To doesn't make it back, then what? We might be killed right then and there!'

'Then we sure as hell better hope he does win. I'd hate to think we lasted this long only to be shot in the back of the head!'

The Sioux army began moving away, families making a low moaning sound, their traditional way of praying for victory and a safe return. Kee-To raised his rifle high over his head, acknowledging their prayers, as the long line of warriors started uphill. His thoughts now turned only on finding the horse soldiers and killing every single one of them, especially this white man who led them if he had that chance.

Far over the intervening mountains, Colonel Greenwood called Loy Marvel to his tent that same morning. One quick look at the officer's drawn face was all it took to see he was on the edge of another loud rant of displeasure.

'Where in God's name is Quiet Eye? He's been gone far too long without returning. I need that information about the trail the tribes took. Do I have to send you out to find him, too!' Greenwood's face twisted in anger.

Loy shook his head. 'No tellin' where he is by now. Somethin' might have happened to him.'

'Happened to him? He's disappeared without a trace, that's what's happened to him, and just when I needed him most.'

'I can ride out and try to find his trail, but you'd be on your own here if I did.'

Greenwood paced back and forth, cussing under his breath, trying to decide what to do next. He turned to Marvel, running a hand through his thick, white hair. 'I can't let you do that. You'll have to stay, as much as I need that information. If the young fool has wandered off and got himself killed, so be it!'

CHAPTER NINE

The Sioux army charged up the mountains with the white hot heat of battle burning deep in their chests, eager to find the cavalrymen to adorn their lodges with many fresh scalps of their hated enemy. Kee-To had instilled his own ferocity into each and every one of his warriors that this battle, above all others, must be the one to destroy the horse soldiers so completely they would withdraw from all Sioux lands never to return again.

The long ride to the top was shortened by several days because of the wild enthusiasm of the braves, who drove their horses relentlessly higher. Reaching the top, Iron Hand ordered Quiet Eye to point the direction he'd taken when leaving the cavalry camp. By staying along the knife-edge ridges, the huge band of warriors could make better time than fighting their way up and down steep canyons deep in snow drifts. It also meant that once they reached the soldiers, going into battle their horses and the Sioux themselves would be in better shape physically to begin the brutal assault, and they would hold a second edge by coming down on top of the enemy, not at their level or from below.

Loy Marvel was called to Colonel Greenwood's tent a second time and ordered to leave camp and ride for the top to learn how much further they would have to struggle to reach the summit. After saddling up and taking extra grub, the scout pushed his horse hard for three more days before icy peaks came into view close above. Upon reaching them he made a sparse camp, intending to stay just overnight before starting back down. He had worried about Quiet Eye's disappearance since it became obvious something had happened to the young scout. The Pawnee tracker might not have had the experience of Loy, but he considered him able enough to carry out the orders he'd been given and return in a week or so at the most. That worry about his fate had nagged at Marvel constantly after he'd vanished without a trace.

The whinnying of a horse woke Loy after a freezing cold night in his small tent. He was anxious to saddle up and start back down for camp and hot meals. Throwing off his one thin wool blanket, he pulled on boots and twisted into a jacket, pushing the tent flap open to step outside. Suddenly he found himself facing Kee-To Iron Hand and a dozen warriors all leveling rifles on him. Marvel was so stunned he couldn't cry out. Instead, he slowly raised his hands, staring back at the Sioux while being disarmed, until he saw Quiet Eye, hands tied behind his back, guarded by more braves. Once he found his voice, he tried talking fast to save himself from being killed where he stood. He quickly recognized Iron

Hand from all the tales he'd heard describing the savage leader of the Sioux Nation.

'Listen, chief, I hope you understand some American, because I don't mean no harm to you or your people. I ain't no soldier. You gotta believe me. Ask Quiet Eye about that, he'll tell you. I'm only paid to lead the cavalry, not fight with 'em. And I'll tell you something else, too. . . .'

Kee-To held up his hand for Marvel to stop talking. Stepping closer, nearly nose to nose with the old scout, he asked a pointed question. 'Where are horse soldiers?'

Loy was amazed he could speak any English at all. His whiskered face showed his obvious surprise.

'They're on down the mountain,' he pointed, staring back as if hypnotized.

'How far?'

'Ah . . . maybe three days.'

'How many soldiers?'

'I . . . ain't sure. Maybe . . . a hundred or so.'

'They have wagons and cannon, too?'

Loy nodded. 'Yeah, two wagons and a 12-pounder.'

Kee-To quickly ordered his braves to tie Marvel's hands behind his back, boosting him up on his horse. He and the rest of the Sioux mounted their horses, with Kee-To ordering the scout brought up alongside him.

'You show the way to white soldiers.'

Loy didn't answer this time. He knew he had no other choice. Beyond Kee-To and his braves the scout glanced up along a ridge behind his tent camp. That's when his eyes feel on an endless line of mounted warriors, sitting in their horses, starting to ride down to join their vaunted leader. Without uttering another word, the old scout knew the fight to come was going to be a slaughter, and he was already certain the Sioux would not be on the losing end of it. They had every advantage in their favor, unexpected surprise, choice of timing to attack, and riding down from above on top of soldiers below. Marvel glanced at Quiet Eye, both scouts already beginning to wonder if they'd be killed before reaching the cavalry camp. If so, they were now living the last few hours of their lives.

All that day and the next, the Sioux army reined their horses steadily downhill through deep snow and isolated pockets of timber. By the second evening, Kee-To called for the two cavalry scouts to be brought before him again.

'How far are soldiers, now?' He asked.

Marvel took in a deep breath, trying to come up with an answer that made sense. 'I'd have to guess ... by tomorrow, maybe you'd reach them. But I've been gone a while so I can't be sure.'

Kee-To ordered the pair taken away before calling several of his men over while he began formulating a plan. Once again he chose his trusted friend, Running Horse, to carry it out.

'Take six braves and ride downhill tonight. Move like the shadows, slow and quiet. You must not be heard or seen. Find the soldier camp. Learn how many there are and where they keep their horses. I will wait for your return.'

The battle-scarred older chief nodded without answering. He had his orders and knew how important the mission he'd been tasked to carry out was. Choosing his men quickly, Running Horse saddled up. In moments the small band of riders were lost in dark timber, disappearing downhill.

Loy Marvel and Quiet Eye watched them go, both tied hand and foot, seated against a pine tree and guarded by four Sioux braves. Iron Hand walked back to his pair of captives. 'Tomorrow we will attack and kill all the white soldiers. You two will stay here.'

Marvel cleared the lump in his throat, staring up at Kee-To. 'Are you gonna . . . kill us, too?' He forced the out the question.

Iron Hand did not answer. He studied the pair intently for a few seconds longer before walking away, leaving both men with their hearts pounding in their throats.

Even in full darkness, the night-time glow of snow reflected enough light and made it possible for Running Horse and his braves to work their way down until, hours later, he held up his hand to stop. Somewhere below, he caught a faint whiff of smoke wafting up through the trees. A moment later he heard the distant whinnying of horses. He'd found the cavalry camp! Motioning his men off their horses, they crept lower through broken timber until they saw small campfires still smoldering and tents scattered throughout a large clearing. The chief carefully studied the layout, especially noting there were no night guards on the edge of camp, or on three lines of horses picketed back of camp. After fifteen minutes more he signaled his braves to retreat back uphill to their horses. Just as he turned to leave, he saw a tall, thin soldier step out of his tent, lighting a cigar. In the flickering flame of his match, Running Horse could see the man had snow white hair nearly down to his shoulders. He would remember that strange-looking white man and tell Kee-To of him, too.

The sky had yet to show any hint of dawn before Running Horse was back up in the Sioux camp. As promised, Kee-To had not slept, waiting up instead for his friend's return and the vital information he'd hoped to hear. The old chief quickly filled him in on the entire layout of the cavalry camp, drawing it out in snow with a stick. He pointed out their many tents, the picket line of horses, finishing with a remark about the strange, white haired soldier he'd seen.

'He is old, with long, white hair. I have never seen a white man like that. He may be the one who leads them because of his age.'

'I will learn this from the scouts we have captured. If he is their leader, I will kill him first, myself. You have done well, old friend. I will prepare our warriors tomorrow. Before these soldiers have left their sleeping tents, we will ride down on them the next morning with a great victory for all the Sioux Nation!'

The cavalry camp was still sleeping as the first gray streaks of dawn lit the surrounding pines heavily laden in snow. Captain Stodlmeyer sat up on his cot, shivering in long underwear against the bitter cold, wondering if this would be another day filled with the kind of misery he and the men had suffered by Colonel Greenwood's refusal to listen to his or anyone else's advice. Loy Marvel was gone, trying to learn what happened to Quiet Eye. Now he had not returned either. Without either scout to lead them, Stodlmeyer knew the entire campaign could only end up in disaster. Still the colonel would not consider turning back or changing his plan. The captain prepared himself for another major confrontation this morning, trying to talk Greenwood into stopping to assess the dire situation.

Pulling on his pants and shirt, he slipped into cold boots, and stood twisting into a heavy jacket, adjusting a wide-brimmed hat on his head. Stepping outside the tent, he tied a yellow bandana around his neck, starting for the colonel's tent by crunching through the snow. Reaching it, he called out.

'Are you up, sir?'

'Yes, I'm up, Stodlmeyer, and it's time for the bugler to blow wake-up call. After you do that, I want you back here. I want to discuss something with you.'

'All right, sir, I'll be right back.'

Stodlmeyer ordered the bugler out of his tent, cold bugle in hand, to begin the piercing notes for troopers to rise. He brought the brass instrument to his lips, sounding out the call, as cavalrymen began exiting their tents, some still slipping into jackets and hats, trying to fully wake up. As Stodlmeyer turned to walk back to Greenwood's tent, he looked up to see a sudden avalanche of snow cascading down on the camp through tall pines. It took only another instant to realize the white wave was driven by an endless line of Sioux riders, charging down shouting war cries, firing rifles and pistols, shattering the icy air in an endless thunder of sudden death. Troopers ran back for their tents, fumbling madly for weapons, but too late to turn back the overwhelming attack. Already Sioux horses and riders were sweeping in among the tents and men, killing cavalrymen at pistol range.

Stodlmeyer pulled his pistol, running and firing at the same time at dark shadows swirling around him, while sprinting for the colonel's tent. As he reached it, Greenwood burst out, wild eyed in panic. Before he could fire a shot, Stodlmeyer literally tackled him, driving both of them back inside the tent. They crashed to the floor as the wave of riders swept over the tent and flattened it under a pile of snow. Outside, they heard the screams and cries of men dying between the furious gunfire still going on. Greenwood struggled, trying to get the captain off from on top of him, but Stodlmeyer pinned him down so he could not move.

'Let me up, damn you!' he ordered, still trying to twist loose.

'Shut up and lay still. You get outside you're a dead man, you understand me. There's nothing either of us can do. It's too late for that!'

Finally, when it seemed the killing and firing would never end, the shooting began to subside as warriors rode through the camp, executing the wounded and dying one at a time. Kee-To reined his horse through flattened tents and dead bodies, a smoking-hot pistol still in his hand, looking for the soldier with white hair. Running Horse rode up alongside him, two bloody scalps hanging from his horse, the look of victory clear on his lined face.

'Where is the soldier with white hair?' Iron Hand asked.

Running Horse pulled his horse in a slow circle, surveying the shattered camp. 'I did not see him. Maybe he is dead. I will look for him.'

The old chief spent the next half hour riding among dead bodies sprawled in the snow. At the few tents still standing, riddled with bullet holes, he got down off his horse, seeing what or who was inside. None held the man with white hair. Riding back to Kee-To, he reported not finding that man. Iron Hand slid his pistol back in his waistband, with new orders to round up all the rifles, pistols and ammunition his braves could carry, before preparing to leave.

'A small number of horse soldiers ran off into trees when we attacked. Should I send braves after them?'

'No,' Kee-To shook his head. 'They will be dead men quickly. Without horses they will not go far. The wolves will have them. Burn the wagons. Leave the cannon. It will turn to rust.'

Neither Kee-To or Running Horse could know that not more than thirty feet away the soldier with long white hair and his captain lay still, barely afraid to breath, as the sound of horses' hoofs and talk of Sioux victory swirled around them. When those sounds finally faded away, and black smoke billowed up through the surrounding pines, the two men cautiously dug their way out from under the buried tent. Greenwood grunted to his feet, getting his first look at the bloody disaster surrounding him. He could not believe what his eyes said was true. His throat choked with emotion. He couldn't speak for several moments, knowing he and his orders had been the reason for a military disaster of unparalleled proportions. He turned to Stodlmeyer, tears beginning to fill his eyes.

'How . . . how could this happen . . . to me?' his shoulders sank with his voice, the captain stepping up alongside him.

'It's not just you, sir. Think of all the men lost.'

'That's because . . . it was a sneak attack. Not a man-to-man . . . fight. That yellow coward would not face me in a . . . real battle!'

Stodlmeyer did not answer this time. It was already clear to him the colonel was beginning to form an alibi for his crushing defeat. He'd have to face his superior officers back at Fort Riley with that excuse and whatever else he could dream up. First he, the colonel, and whatever men still remained alive, had to find enough horses to begin the grueling ride back down out of these deadly mountains, trying to make the long, dangerous trip back to the stockade, if they even could reach it.

'It looks like the Sioux took most of the horses,' Stodlmeyer said. 'We might not be able to find more than only a few.'

'Just be sure you find enough for you and me. If the others have to walk, there's nothing I can do about that. I want to leave this stink of death as soon as possible.'

Stodlmeyer looked at Greenwood incredulously. He could not believe that after this disaster he could actually care so little about what few men survived, let alone those already dead.

*

As the shattered remains of the colonel and his men began the long march down out of the Blue Cloud Mountains, Kee-To, Iron Hand and his victorious warriors topped the high peaks ready to start down for the village far below. He pulled to a halt with one final decision to make. He still had Loy Marvel and Quiet Eye to deal with. He did not want to reveal the location of his village by taking them down with him. He motioned they be brought up alongside him and their hands untied. Marvel stiffened in the saddle, fearing they were both about to be shot dead. Kee-To began speaking loud enough so all the warriors around him could hear his words.

'These two are free to go. They cannot go back to the horse soldiers. They will have to find another way. They cannot ride with us, either.' He turned his gaze on the two men. 'Go now, before I change my mind and let my warriors have you.'

Marvel looked over at Quiet Eye. 'Come on boy, let's get kicking while we can. We'll find our way out of these damn mountains on our own, and still have our hair left!'

When Iron Hand and his warriors burst out of timber above their village, children ran toward them waving and shouting, as women and old men followed. Many braves hung fresh scalps from lances or tied on saddles, celebrating their great victory with wild war cries. That evening, large fires leaped high into the night sky, while circles of braves danced and whirled, their sweaty bodies glistening in firelight, to the endless beating of drums. Yet Kee-To sat watching his men without a

125

flicker of emotion in his dark eyes. He had forged a great victory over the hated white soldiers, but now darker thoughts played across his mind. He knew once word of the soldiers' defeat reached the ears of other white chiefs in far away lands they would launch another army against him and a larger one to search out and extract revenge on all the Sioux. Soon enough Iron Hand would have to either face them again, or conjure up a way for him and all his people to avoid being killed, jailed or hung. The white man would not take this defeat and retreat. They'd only return in greater numbers. He was as certain of that as dawn would rise again over the Blue Cloud Mountains.

A military board of inquiry was called two months later at Fort Riley to investigate the slaughter that took place at the hands of Kee-To, Iron Hand. Colonel Milford Greenwood's command actions and decisions were to be closely questioned. The colonel knew the result could be that he might not only lose his command, but possibly be discharged from the army if the board members voted against him. His tragic defeat had even made newspaper headlines all the way back east in New York and especially Washington, where the political fallout was already taking place at the army's general headquarters. Captain Stodlmeyer, as the colonel's second in command, was also ordered to make the trip south to Fort Riley to give his testimony. The seven board members to conduct the hearing, all military men of long experience, had all faced other Indian tribes in battle. They were lead by General Rutherford Alonzo Seaton.

Colonel Greenwood had many intense private conversations with Captain Stodlmeyer on their long train ride south. He'd made it abundantly clear that if the captain's statements to the board left any shred of doubt that his decisions leading up to the Sioux attack were in question, the colonel would personally see to it that Stodlmeyer never rose another rank in the cavalry, regardless of how long he stayed in the military. The captain had no doubt that Greenwood meant every single word of it.

On a cold, blustery winter Monday morning the board was convened, coming to order by General Seaton's gavel ringing sharply down off its hardwood base. The low, log building was cold and clammy, even with a large pot-bellied stove over in one corner snapping and belching to fresh kindling. The general read the time and purpose of the meeting, everything to be said taken down by a scribe seated at the far end of the long table, pen and inkwell nearby. Greenwood cleared his throat and sat up ramrod straight, preparing himself for the most important two days in his life, with the board's final decision to be announced the following afternoon.

Board members began their questioning, taking turns with insightful, probing questions, moving down the table, one officer at a time. When asked why he insisted on trying to bring heavily loaded supply wagons up into snow-laden mountains, the colonel had a quick answer, he'd already anticipated.

'I knew the Sioux leader, he's called Kee-To, Iron Hand, had taken control of all the tribes. That meant he'd have hundreds of warriors at his disposal. I surmised I'd have a long drawn out campaign trying to find and engage him. That meant many weeks or longer on the trail, far from our outpost. I needed those supplies to keep my men well fed and ready to take the fight to the savage. As far as I was concerned, I had no other choice.'

The military men leaned forward on their elbows as more questions were put to the colonel while they weighed his answers. Another questioned his wisdom at trying to pull an unwieldy, 12-pound cannon into the same country. Greenwood had a quick answer for that one, too.

'I knew when we finally caught up to the Sioux I could be facing a field battle where the number of Indians matched the men under my command. Under circumstances such as that, a shelling with the 12-pounder could quickly turn the tide of battle in our favor. The Sioux had only hand weapons. That meant they had to get close in to fight on foot or horses. With the cannon, I could bombard them from a distance and kill many of them before they could close in. As far as I was concerned, the cannon was a piece I could not go into battle without.'

General Seaton had studied Greenwood carefully throughout his questioning, weighing the colonel's words and answers. Now he began questions of his own.

'Colonel, you and your command were overrun at dawn by this Sioux leader you call Iron Hand and his braves. Why did you not have night guards posted around your camp to deter such a devastating attack from ever taking place? You were admittedly in hostile country and conditions. It's common military knowledge that officers always protect themselves and their men this way. Yet you ignored this basic rule. I'd be very interested to hear your answer to that, sir.'

Greenwood didn't hesitate. 'My answer, General, is two fold. First, we were not following the same trail the tribes took up into the Blue Cloud Mountains. I'd elected to take an easier route several miles away. To me, that meant there was no chance we'd run into the Sioux, who were fleeing from us for the tops to get away. Second, I'd had the misfortune to lose both my scouts and had no knowledge of that part of the mountains we were in. I did elect to stop for several days while I reconnoitered before going further. I was about to send Captain Stodlmeyer out with a party of men trying to see exactly how far we had to climb to reach the top of the mountains. Then I meant to follow the high country back until I found where the Sioux had crossed over, and sweep down on them from above. They attacked me on that very morning, so I did not have the opportunity to carry it out.'

Seaton stared back at Greenwood through pale, blue eyes. He had another question. 'Your second in command, Captain Stodlmeyer, had repeatedly tried to warn you of the dangers of wearing your men out with pointless labor and orders, until they were no longer the fighting force they should have been. Forcing men, even deserters, to walk through deep snow is criminal, and doubling up mounted troopers for extra horses laboring to pull heavy wagons and cannon makes no sense. Every officer at this table understands that a superior officer is in command to be obeyed, but a good officer also considers what his second has to say and, if it has merit, act upon it. You did neither. Your treatment of the deserters alone could put you in a court martial confrontation. No officer worthy of the name would treat any man or men under him in that way, regardless of the charges that might be brought against them.'

'Those four had committed the worst offense any cavalrymen can make. They tried to desert me at a time when battle was imminent. I felt no need to make their lives easier because of it!' Greenwood's voice rose to almost a shout for the first time, 'and I would add that Captain Stodlmeyer repeatedly opposed my orders and even thought this Sioux leader was nearly invincible. With a second like that, I had almost no help at all. The command suffered because of it.'

The room fell to stunned silence at the colonel's emotional outburst. The general still stood, studying the officer, noticing how quickly he always had an answer to any question asked. It was almost as if he'd rehearsed them in advance so he could give rapid-fire replies while trying to sound spontaneous. The utter cruelty Greenwood had exhibited was most troubling of all.

Colonel Greenwood was finally excused and Captain Stodlmeyer was called forward to be sworn in. That's when Seaton made an unusual request. He asked the colonel to leave the room and retire to his quarters while the captain testified. He did not want Stodlmeyer's answers subject to possible pressure by the colonel's presence. The general hoped he might provide key answers he and the board had not yet heard. Other panel members were eager to continue and so he sat back letting them proceed.

CHAPTER TEN

Captain Stodlmeyer was assured by General Seaton that everything he said during questioning would be kept in the strictest confidence by himself and all board members. However, the captain had been in the horse soldiers long enough to know that decisions made on a case of this magnitude, and the testimony of men who made it, never stayed secret for long. The tragic loss of life of men under Colonel Greenwood's command was common knowledge throughout the army and had made major east coast newspaper headlines. He was certain his testimony would eventually be leaked too, and that meant Colonel Greenwood would hear of it. It would just be a matter of time before he carried out his promised threat.

Board members, and especially the general, close questioned Stodlmeyer about certain command decisions Greenwood had made, why he'd made them, and if he'd ever questioned or disagreed with any of them. The captain moved uneasily in the chair. His disagreements with Greenwood were known openly by many of the men who'd survived the Sioux attack. He had to walk and talk a fine line between what he knew to be truth, yet not tell every single event they'd argued heatedly over.

The general was especially insistent on why the colonel had tried to take such burdensome wagons and the artillery piece up into steep mountains and deep snow. He questioned Stodlmeyer closely on that point more than once over the next hour.

'All I can answer, General, is that Colonel Greenwood felt he had to have both backing us up on the long trailing we were doing trying to find Kee-To, Iron Hand.'

'You did disagree with his decision, did you not, and more than once?'

'Yes . . . I did bring it up. But he was my superior officer, so I tried not to make a habit out of it and make things even worse.'

'Can you tell me how the colonel managed to lose both his scouts?'

'I do not know the answer to that and I don't think anyone else does either.'

'In this case you'd be wrong. Would it surprise you to know that Loy Marvel and his Pawnee counterpart rode safely out of the Blue Cloud Mountains several weeks ago and into one of our outposts?'

'You mean they're both alive?'

'Yes, they are. They were both captured by this Sioux leader and for some unexplainable reason turned loose after the attack on Greenwood's command. I still cannot understand why this savage would do something like that. Can you?'

'I do not know, sir. I'm amazed to hear either one

132

made it out, but I'm certainly glad to know they did.'

'Marvel has said he believed Colonel Greenwood to be a stubborn officer who drove his men needlessly on a mission that was fraught with disaster from the very first day they left your outpost. Do you believe that statement to be an exaggeration of the facts, or would you agree with it?'

Stodlmeyer paused, gathering his thoughts, while trying to avoid a direct comparison. 'I . . . wouldn't put it exactly in those terms, sir. I would say the colonel is a man of his own convictions, right or wrong, who was sent into country he'd never seen or fought in before. Especially not against an adversary like Iron Hand. He was trying to take him on in his own ground. That stacked the odds against him from the start. Losing both our scouts only made it that much more difficult.'

The panel continued asking questions for the next three-quarters of an hour until they were satisfied they'd heard enough and General Seaton rose to speak again.

'You are a very smart young man, Captain. I appreciate what you're trying to do, but this board will make its decision and call both you and Colonel Greenwood back tomorrow afternoon with our findings. You are excused, for this session.'

A weak winter sun screened by low clouds driven by cold winds set the mood for the entire next day. In mid-afternoon, both officers were called back into the hearing room and seated. The general came to his feet, a single sheet of papers in his hand, while all board members stared straight ahead at the two men without any outward show of emotion. Seaton cleared his throat, preparing to speak. For a moment longer, he studied the pair of officers.

'It is the findings of this military board of inquiry that Colonel Milford Greenwood led his men on a mission of self-inflicted disasters, not the least of which was the tragic loss of men under his command, against the Sioux Nation. That loss cannot be excused or explained away by any logical explanation. His many judgments have been found to be woefully inadequate of a field officer going into battle that led directly to the defeat of his entire command structure. These glaring errors were many, including bogging down the command by insisting on taking heavily loaded wagons and even a 12-pound artillery piece up into steep snow-clad mountains. Another major failure that led to his defeat and that of his men was not posting night guards around his camp or horses, leaving the entire command at the mercy of attacking Sioux. The unconscionable and outright cruelty of forcing soldiers, even deserters, to be put afoot walking through deep snow where it was obvious they could not survive was beyond all bounds of military code of conduct. It is therefore concluded by this board and myself that Colonel Milford Greenwood be reduced in rank to that of corporal, losing his command. He will be under the authority of officers above him if he wishes to remain in the army. That decision is his alone to make. We have given him this choice only because of his years serving in the army prior to moving his men north to engage Kee-To, Iron Hand. It is my order that should Corporal Milford Greenwood remain in the service he will never be given the position to lead other men again. This tribunal is closed.'

Greenwood sat stunned at the findings. His face reddened with anger, then a deeper tone of humiliation. He swallowed hard, staring straight ahead, until the board members seated facing him only became indistinct blurs. His dreams of rising in command after capturing Kee-To, Iron Hand, had come crashing down around him like a crushing weight. He barely heard Captain Stodlmeyer's assessment from the panel as the general delivered it.

'This board also finds that Captain Austin Vance Stodlmeyer acted in accordance with military law, even when he'd continually argued for changes that might have averted the disaster that befell the men under Greenwood's command. His role in this entire debacle is deemed blameless, and quite to the contrary, his actions during the attack very likely saved the former colonel's life. Therefore we will now be ordering that his rank be elevated to colonel, and his position in the northern outpost where he has served be continued. The fact-finding mission of this hearing is now closed. Both men will receive necessary paperwork with our conclusions and recommendations.'

General Seaton brought the gavel down with a resounding crack, but he wasn't really finished just yet. Greenwood had been obsessed with tracking down the charismatic Sioux leader and bringing him back in chains. He'd failed miserably and left a bloody stain on Western Command that the general deeply felt, too. Now the same compelling reason that drove Greenwood fixed itself in the mind of General Seaton. In the weeks ahead he would marshal the single largest number of cavalrymen ever brought together for a single engagement, molding them into two separate armies. He was going back to the Blue Cloud Mountains to redeem the name of his command, while finally bringing Kee-to, Iron Hand to justice in his own court here at Fort Riley.

Seaton was back in his office after the hearing when there was a knock on the door. Looking up from the board's paperwork, he called out for whoever it was to come in. When the door opened, he was amazed to see Milford Greenwood step inside, hat in hand.

'The hearing is over and the board and myself have made our decision. Nothing you can say now will change that, if that's what you came here for.' The general stared back.

'It is not, sir. If my years in the cavalry have meant anything I want to ask just one favor of you.'

'Favor? I don't believe you're in any position to ask for favors, corporal.'

'Please hear me out, sir. I know I no longer have any command authority, but I want to ask to be included as an observer and nothing more in the armies you're bringing together. I want to ride back into the Blue Cloud Mountains and watch this Sioux murderer taken down once and for all. I have lost everything else, including my dignity, self-respect and command. I have nothing left. I'm begging you to let me ride along with you.'

The general came to his feet, studying the once proud officer, considering his surprising request. It was obvious that Greenwood had been reduced to a shell of a man. Seaton took no joy in seeing it. He took in a long breath, considering his plea.

'I will allow you to ride with us, but only as a second to Colonel Stodlmeyer. You will neither suggest nor give orders to anyone, enlisted men or officers. Is that clearly understood?'

'It is, and I thank you for it. I only want to be there when you kill or capture Kee-To, Iron Hand.'

'I will inform Colonel Stodlmeyer you will be riding with us. He certainly spent enough time riding with you before. I'm sure he won't mind doing so now, even though your roles have been reversed and you will take orders from him.'

Far away over snowy peaks, the Sioux still endlessly rejoiced in their great victory over the horse soldiers. Each night roaring fires snapped, flames reaching for the sky, as warriors told and retold of the slaughter of the white invaders. Only one Sioux sat in deep thought of what might come next, and there was no joy in what he saw. Kee-To finally decided, calling his chiefs to council and telling them of his deep concerns.

'While our people are happy to dance and sing their praises to Spirit Warriors, I have seen a dark cloud coming over the mountains sounding thunder, bringing lightning down on us. That thunder is guns.'

'How can that be,' Running Horse questioned. 'We have crushed the soldiers completely. They will never return here again. Their dead lie under winter snow at this moment. No soldier comes to mourn them.'

'Yes, in battle we have defeated them. But there are many more soldiers in other places where we have never been or fought. They will all be brought here against us. The white man will not give up and ride away. We must prepare for it with a plan.'

'What plan?' Buffalo Horn spoke up. 'Our people have suffered enough. I say we are safe and will no longer have to fight to live. Can you not hear their singing and the beating of drums of victory?'

'I can hear them. But they do not know what I have seen in a vision.'

The chiefs looked at each other, wondering if such an event could actually take place. Hawk's Eye spoke first this time.

'We know your visions with the Ancient Ones are true. But where would you take us if such a thing happens? We have left our villages far behind to come to this place so soldiers would not find us. There is no place left for us to go.'

'There is such a place . . . Canada Land.' Iron Hand announced to the stunned chiefs.

'Can-a-da?' Many Sons mouthed the strange word slowly. 'That land is far away. None of us have ever been there. We do not know what trails to take or how many rivers to cross. Why would we want our people to be forced to leave again?'

'We hold two white trappers. Canada Land is their home. They will show us the way.' Kee-To stared back at his chiefs.

While the four leaders began talking among themselves, Kee-To ordered the white men be brought before them. Gerard Manley and Lonn Story were marched in minutes later by three guards. Their tattered clothes and gaunt faces showed the endless work they'd been forced to do on skimpy rations. Both wondered, without asking, why they'd been so suddenly summoned before the Sioux leaders. That answer came quickly with Iron Hand's first question.

'You know the way north . . . to Canada Land?'

Manley glanced at Story, with an odd look on his face before answering. 'Yes, we do. That is our home. We hope to live to see it again, as our two friends have.'

'How far is this place from here?'

'Ah . . . maybe three weeks' ride,' Story spoke up.

Kee-To explained the answer to the chiefs, who spoke little English, before turning back to the two men. 'You show me the way, maybe soon.'

Before either could answer, Kee-To made a quick nod to the guards, who quickly pulled the pair away. The moment they were gone, he looked around the circle of Sioux.

'These two white men can take us to Canada, where the horse soldiers cannot follow. At last our people can put up their teepees and not be forced to leave. I will send our braves to watch over the soldiers' log walls. If the white men gather there to make war, we will leave this place never to return. Some of you wanted to kill the two white trappers. Now you know why I did not.'

Ten Sioux scouts made the dangerous, time-consuming journey to country back near the cavalry stockade, spying on the compound from nearby hills while keeping themselves hidden. Days passed into two weeks with little more than normal activity, until one afternoon when an endless line of cavalrymen, pack mules and wagons suddenly came into view coming up the canyon below and heading for the outpost. Gray Antelope, leader of the Sioux band, crept to the snowy edge of a drop-off counting the long line of soldiers riding by below. He pulled back quickly, ordering the rest of his men to break camp and saddle up. They had the long ride back over the Blue Cloud Mountains to inform Kee-To his vision had been true. The sooner he knew of it, the sooner all the tribes would either have to face more fighting and hardship or flee. The land their ancient forefathers had found and settled in was slipping away mile by bloody mile. They had no choice left but to leave it all behind or die trying to stay to defend it.

The staging area for General Seaton's huge force of men, horses and supplies became a beehive of constant activity. Preparing to move it all into the mountains to find and crush the Sioux leader and his people meant Seaton had to carefully school his officers on his plan of attack. Standing in front of a large map hung on the wall of his office, he began explaining his two-pronged approach without noticing a shadowy figure who entered the back of the room, quietly taking a seat. Corporal Greenwood had come to listen to the general's remarks on strategy, and a question only he knew to ask.

'I propose to trap and finish off this Indian leader Kee-To, Iron Hand, by using two separate platoons of one hundred men each. I will have Colonel Stodlmeyer take the first platoon and follow the original trail the Sioux made going up and over the Blue Cloud

Mountains. He's been in that country before and is familiar with what he's up against, plus the timeline evolved. I'll take the second platoon and skirt the mountains to the west, until I find a low point to hook around and start up the backside of the range.

'We will want to engage the Sioux at the same moment, which means we'll both have our scouts out front looking to make contact with each other and coordinate timing as we close in on him. Then we'll attack, trapping the tribes between us in a withering crossfire. He'll have no escape this time. Our men here have had sufficient time to put up supplies. I propose we should be ready to ride in three days. Are there any questions?'

Greenwood's hand went up. For the first time the general looked beyond the front row of officers as the corporal stood up. Every man in the room turned to see who it was, while Seaton pondered if he should even entertain a question from his ex-colonel after his colossal failure. After a moment's hesitation, he decided to do so.

'Yes, what is it, Corporal Greenwood?'

'I'd like to ask to ride along with you when you leave. I would like to be there when you take Iron Hand down once and for all. I've been reduced to where I am because of him. I'd like to see him go down, too.'

A buzz of whispers went through the room as the officers turned back to the general to see what he'd say about the sudden unexpected request. Seaton lowered the map pointer, tapping it slowly in his other hand. His eyes went to Colonel Stodlmeyer sitting in the front row, trying to read his reaction. He saw none. The general took in a slow breath, preparing to answer.

'If Colonel Stodlmeyer will have you, in no official capacity of course, I'll consider your request. It's up to him. Colonel?' He turned his attention back to the newly appointed officer.

Stodlmeyer slowly nodded his approval, remembering how their roles had been so suddenly reversed and the ongoing shame Greenwood suffered because of it.

'So be it, then. Corporal, you will report to the colonel for your orders, if he has any. We'll have one more meeting before we leave. For now this session is adjourned.'

Long before the hard-riding Sioux scouts had reached their village, General Seaton and his long line of cavalry-men had already left the log-walled compound and were on the march making their way toward the Blue Cloud Mountains. They moved swiftly without the burden of heavy wagons and artillery pieces. Instead, Seaton had wisely ordered food, ammunition and other supplies be carried on sturdy mules that could keep up with the horses. He reached the foot of the mountains in half the time it had taken Colonel Greenwood to accomplish. The moment they crossed Three Rivers the general split the force in two as he'd planned. Colonel Stodlmeyer was ordered to immediately begin the climb toward the top following the original trail Kee-To had taken weeks earlier.

'The faster we both move, the less time Iron Hand will have to realize we have him in a box when we find him and attack. Remember to order your scouts to stay well out ahead of you so they can make contact with mine, while I work my way around the other side of these mountains. We'll meet then. Good hunting!' The two men exchanged salutes before parting.

Kee-To waited with deep concern for his braves to return from spying on the outpost and what they might find. When the riders came slipping and sliding down the mountain at a breakneck pace to spill out their story his worst fears were realized. He immediately called his chiefs to council, ordering them to prepare their people to take down their teepees, load up goods and prepare to move, en mass, once again. It took another three days before the tribes had everything on horses, dogs and travois mounted up ready to leave. Kee-To called for Manley and Story to be put on horses and brought up to him. Both men were astonished to see the huge band of hundreds of Sioux lined up behind their leader on horses and afoot. Before either could speak, Iron Hand gave them an order.

'You show the way to Canada land. We leave now!'

It took another moment before Manley could speak up. 'You want us to take all your people north over the border?'

'All of them. We go now. Ride fast. Don't stop!'

Colonel Stodlmeyer had followed the old Sioux trail up the mountains, making good time even though steep climbing was hard on men and horses. Once over the top and well down the far side, his scouts ran into General Seaton's scouts, assuring the colonel that Seaton was only three days behind them and coming fast. Stodlmeyer proposed to hold his men where they were until Seaton came closer before both forces could proceed farther down to where they believed the Sioux village might be. His written communiqué taken back to the general carefully spelled this out.

While Stodlmeyer and his men rested, Kee-To was already moving north as fast as he could push his hundreds of followers. It didn't take long for the blistering pace to begin leaving those on foot, older men and women carrying babies, farther behind. He rode back trying to encourage them to keep up or shed some of the load they were carrying. For the first week it seemed to help but even in diminishing snow they fell back again, leaving Kee-To to worry about how to protect them. He was desperate to come up with something.

Far behind, General Seaton and Colonel Stodlmeyer's forces reached the opposite ends of the valley, prepared to attack where the village had stood. As they rode out of timber toward each other both men were left speechless at finding only hundreds of empty stone fire pits and a scattering of teepee poles standing dark and silent against a snowy background. When they met, the general sat in the saddle, stunned he'd been outsmarted just like all the other cavalrymen sent against Iron Hand, and even worse, without firing a single shot. His face reddened as he sucked in a deep breath of icy air, looking around at the abandoned encampment in disgust before speaking.

'I'll run this savage down if I have to ride through the gates of hell to do so!' His strained voice was almost a shout. His next order was to send his scouts out to find the trail the Sioux had taken leaving the valley and how long they'd been gone. In less than an hour the two trackers were back with an answer.

'They've gone north, sir. The whole bunch of them,' one scout answered.

'North? North to where?'

'I'm not sure sir, but if they stayed on it long enough it could lead over the Kicking Horse Mountains into Canada.'

'Canada?' The light of realization suddenly dawned on Seaton's face. 'By God, that's where he's trying to go and we've got to stop him. If he reaches there he'll slip away from us for good. We cannot let that happen! Colonel, you and your men will now come under my command. We'll move as one force. We're going after him even if we have to ride these horses until they drop. Pass the word we're going on half rations to make our supplies last long enough. Let's get cracking!'

Behind Stodlmeyer and the general, Corporal Greenwood sat in the saddle, saying nothing and eyeing Seaton's obvious frustration and open anger. Seaton was now getting a bitter taste of the same kind of defeat he'd suffered, losing his command and hard-earned stripes because of it. In some small way he hated to admit even to himself, he took an undeniable measure of pleasure in it. The Sioux leader had done it again and in his immediate victory lessened the shame he had been forced to endure. He hoped silently that the general felt the sting of it as deeply as he had.

CHAPTER ELEVEN

Kee-To pushed Story and Manley unmercifully north, knowing as he did so some of his own people would begin to fall behind. Trying to help them, he sent Running Horse and a number of his braves back to protect and move them forward at a faster pace, if possible. Reaching the far end of the long line, he immediately issued two new orders. First he told those forced to walk to throw away anything not absolutely necessary to survive, lessening their burden. Next he ordered half his men to take anyone, especially the women and small children still on foot, to ride double with them. Old men, the sick and infirm would still have to fend for themselves, as brutal as that choice was.

Running Horse had a third concern and one he and Kee-To had not discussed. Reining his horse to a halt at the end of the line, he looked back towards the Blue Cloud Mountains, deeply worried the horse soldiers might be back there someplace trailing them, coming closer every day. He made a quick decision, summoning his remaining warriors and telling them they would ride back several days to check their trail to be certain they were not being followed. He gave one brave an order before leaving.

'Ride to Kee-To and tell him I will not be gone long. I want to see we are not being followed by white soldiers and attacked while we sleep. Tell him I will catch up to him in a few days. Go quickly.'

The broad, well-trampled trail left by the Sioux could be followed even through the night. Running Horse knew if they were being followed the soldiers could not miss it, as Kee-To had predicted earlier. He pushed his men hard for two more days until he reached an open valley several miles long. The tribes had stopped here to rest themselves and their horses earlier. He ordered his men to make a light camp for a few days' stay in a fringe of tall timber at one end of the valley. If the cavalry was tracking them they'd pass through this valley and ride right into a killing ambush of their own making. The small band of warriors waited without building fires that could give them away for three long days, intently watching the far end of the valley for any sign of movement. Only the low moan of icy winter winds and the raucous squawk of passing blue jays broke the monotonous silence.

By the morning of the fourth day, Running Horse's suspicions had finally calmed down. The Sioux had seen nothing and he decided to break camp and ride hard to catch up to Kee-To. Maybe his worry and that of Iron Hand was only a natural, nagging suspicion that had to be put to rest. Sleeping robes were rolled up and tied on horses, before the small band of men pulled themselves atop their ponies. As they started away, one brave suddenly called out, pointing back toward the far end of the valley.

'Look. Riders are coming!'

The chief immediately ordered his men to dismount and tie off their animals while he crept to the edge of timber, squinting hard at the small, distant figures of men on horses. It only took another moment before he could make out their dark blue uniforms, and his heart began pounding fast and hard in his chest. The soldiers had, indeed, been tracking them all this time. In that same instant of realization he knew he had no choice but to use his small band of warriors to try and stop them, poor as those odds were against so large a force of soldiers.

General Seaton and Colonel Stodlmeyer rode close behind two scouts leading them and the long line of cavalrymen strung out behind. Seaton turned to his colonel with a remark. 'I must admit I'm somewhat amazed we haven't caught up to the Sioux yet, as hard as I've been pushing my men to do so.'

'Well, General, as I've said before, Iron Hand is not just another Indian. He's a master of things like this, moving hundreds of his people long distances in short periods of time. You'd think he attended some military academy, learning the art of warfare, the way he does these things. That's one reason why he's stayed free for so long. He's never an adversary to be taken lightly and it's hard to predict what he'll do next.'

'I have no intention of making that mistake either,

Colonel. But we have him at a decided disadvantage this time. He has to protect all his people, the women and children, not just warriors. That will be his downfall, I can assure you of that.'

'Sir,' one of the scouts turned in the saddle. 'That high country ahead is the Kicking Horse Mountains. I believe the border with Canada lies not far on the other side. If you cannot engage the Sioux before they reach it any fight will be a lot tougher. They'll have the advantage of elevation on us and can choose their way easier because of it. That's a big one to overcome, sir.'

'Then we will have to move faster to be certain that does not happen. Bugler!' Seaton twisted toward one of the man riding right behind him. 'Sound the gallop. We're going forward faster.'

The cold brass instrument had just touched the trooper lips when a sudden volley of murderous rifle fire erupted from the stand of timber just ahead, sounding like a thunderclap of death. One of the lead scouts screamed, falling off his horse, while the bugler was hit next, pitching forward out of the saddle. Seaton shouted in pain, grabbing his arm, from another bullet hit. Stodlmeyer quickly grabbed the general's reins, yanking his animal out of line and kicking hard back through soldiers scattering wildly and riding for their lives, some going down, killed or wounded, by murderous rifle fire.

Behind blue puffs of rifle smoke coming out of timber, Running Horse shouted for his braves to continue reloading and firing as fast as they could, killing as many troopers as possible before they scattered wildly.

Reaching the far end of the valley, finally out of rifle

149

range, Stodlmeyer quickly shouted for the medical officer to attend the general's arm wound. Seaton slid down out of the saddle, grimacing in pain, as the medic ran forward and helped him remove his heavy coat, jacket and shirt before opening his canvas medical bag.

The rest of the troopers were still in disarray from the sudden, savage ambush that had left the scattered bodies of their friends lying in the snow out in the flat behind them. The colonel shouted recall, trying to rally them as they rode in an attempt to bring some order to the chaos. One of the men was Corporal Greenwood, who quickly unsaddled and approached Stodlmeyer, asking if he could help in some way.

'No, you cannot,' Stodlmeyer answered. 'I'll handle the men. Just stay out of the way for now. My first concern is for the general and how badly wounded he is before I do anything else.'

At the opposite end of the valley, Running Horse quickly chose one of his braves to carry a message to Kee-To. 'Tell him the horse soldiers are only four days behind. Tell him I will stay here with my warriors and try to stop them from coming closer. I will hold them as long as I can. Tell him not to wait for us. The soldiers are many and we are few. Take the fastest horse and leave now. Do not stop to rest.'

General Seaton's face twisted in pain. He leaned back seated against a large pine, eyes closed and holding his breath, while the medic carefully cleaned the bloody wound in his upper arm and then began bandaging it. 'The bullet went clear through, General,' the medic said. 'I've stopped the bleeding, but you'll need more care than I can give you out here, and I'll put your arm in a sling to keep you from moving it. You don't want to start it bleeding again. Even riding would be difficult now, sir.'

Seaton looked up at Stodlmeyer with a dark glare, facing the realization he was out of action as far as riding further to find and engage Iron Hand. 'I am going to give you the command, Colonel, as much as I hate to. I'll keep a few men back here with me to make our way back to your outpost. I cannot even lift a pistol like this. We must be fairly close to the Sioux to run into this rear-guard of his. Regroup the men. Attack that band of renegades across the valley from opposite directions. Get them in a crossfire. There can't be that many of them. Once you kill them, ride hard for the Kicking Horse Mountains. Our victory is in your hands now, as much as I wanted it in mine. Don't fail me, Colonel. Not after I've come this far.'

'I won't, sir. Are you sure you'll be all right? It's a long ride to the outpost?'

'I will. The hurt of not being in on the kill is about as painful as this bloody hole in my arm. Overrun those Sioux and get on with it. The pride of the cavalry and my command rides with you. Don't besmirch either one!'

Stodlmeyer brought his men together and attacked Running Horse exactly as Seaton had ordered. The bloody fight was fierce but short lived. The colonel's overwhelming numbers won the day. After ordering a detail to bury the troopers killed in the initial ambush, and the far smaller number lost attacking Running Horse, Stodlmeyer took the rest of his men and started again on the trail left by Kee-To and the tribes moving fast to reach the safety of the border. He rode with renewed vigor. He now had the entire command and every intention of showing he could do the job no other officer had been able to achieve, not even General Seaton himself. He meant to cut off Iron Hand's escape and either kill or capture him in battle, ending the long-held myth that he was unbeatable once and for all.

The lone Sioux messenger reached Kee-To days later after riding day and night. When he told the vaunted chief what had happened it stopped him in his tracks. The loss of his trusted friend and lifelong companion was the bitterest blow of all. Running Horse was gone forever. He'd given his life to stall the advance of the horse soldiers, knowing as he did so he could not stop them. Kee-To turned away for a moment, the news stunning him deeply as if he'd taken a cavalry bullet in the heart. But he could not let even this tragic event stop him. He still had to reach the border and set his people free once and for all. Nothing else mattered. Not even his own death.

Regaining his composure, he ordered Buffalo Horn to take the lead with Manley and Story while he rode back to the end of the long line of Sioux trying to keep pace. They were pitifully strung out near the limit of endurance. Farther back, the dark figures of several old men lay prostrate in the snow. They had nothing left to give but their lives and had already done so. He urged, ordered and shouted for his people not to stop and give up. To do so was death, either by freezing, or the horse soldiers catching up. He swept up one young woman in

152

his arms, carrying her baby wrapped in a blanket around her body. Pulling her close in the saddle, he continued riding up and down the line, demanding his people not to stop.

Two days later they reached the first up thrust of the Kicking Horse Mountains, starting the arduous climb toward the top. Gaining elevation, Kee-To looked back at the lower lands just crossed. Still, they were empty of the horse soldiers. But for how long? Could he and his people reach the final peaks and cross over into Canada without another major battle. He was so close now. After all the struggles and deaths of his people he prayed for the ancient Spirit Warriors to appear and ride by his side these final last miles. He needed their power and wisdom now more than ever before.

The cavalry troopers reached the mountains barely a day behind the fleeing Sioux. Colonel Stodlmeyer had forced his men to ride hard from gray dawn until dark with almost no rest. Men and horses were worn to the bone, their fighting strength diminished, the men's bearded faces gaunt with the lack of sleep and existing on half rations. Stodlmeyer would not give up or give in. He knew he was close. If the Sioux, some even on foot, could travel fast enough to stay ahead of him, so could he and his men overtake them. He refused to believe even Kee-To, Iron Hand, could work a miracle under these brutal conditions. Riding higher three days later, his scout pointed to dark figures lying in the snow just ahead of them.

'What is that?' Stodlmeyer asked as they rode closer.

'It's the bodies of older Sioux that couldn't go any further, sir. They died right here, freezing to death.'

'That means we must be nearly on top of them.' The colonel turned in the saddle, looking behind him. Corporal Greenwood sat two horses back. He eyed the fallen officer a moment, trying to make up his mind about what to do next. He needed someone who had been through this before. He decided to take a chance.

'Corporal, get out of line and up here by my side,' he ordered. Captain Santeen sat next to Stodlmeyer. He turned his attention on him next. 'Captain, I'm going to take a quarter of the men and ride for that low point in the peaks up there. It might take me a while to reach it but I can move faster with fewer men. If I can top out in time we can trap Iron Hand between us and finish him off. Without him leading them his people will collapse. If you hear shooting come on as fast as you can. Be sure to bring plenty of ammo packs, too. This is the last chance we'll have to stop him. If we don't do it now we'll never get another one. You understand the gravity of what I'm saying?'

'I do, sir. I'll push the men even harder than we have.'

'All right, we'll split up here. I'll see you again near the tops. We'll either have Kee-To in irons or dead!'

Kee-To kept a small band of braves riding behind the long moving line of Sioux, struggling higher each day. Upon reaching a promontory, they reined to a stop, looking back down the glistening white slopes. One brave's eyes narrowed suddenly. He uttered a low warning almost under his breath as the others turned, following his pointed hand. Far below, tiny figures of men on horses came into view. All ten warriors quickly yanked their horses around, kicking away to tell Iron Hand what they'd seen. They found him halfway up the line of Sioux as they came riding in with snow flying off their horses' hoofs. Instantly, Kee-To knew it meant trouble. One brave shouted a warning even before pulling to a stop.

'How far back are they?' Iron Hand asked, realizing the battle he'd hoped to avoid had come at the worst time for him and his people.

'They can reach us before we find the top,' one brave answered. 'The soldiers are moving higher, coming fast.'

Kee-To turned away for a moment, his mind racing for an answer. He looked up to the snowy heights still above of him. A canyon broke right away from the line of travel they'd been taking. A second one turned in the opposite direction. It looked like it could lead all the way up to the final peaks. Even as he studied both, a wall of darker, clouds came spilling over the last ridges, driven by a moaning wind mixed with another sound like battle cries from slain Sioux warriors of past wars. The Spirit Warriors were answering Kee-To's earlier prayers for help. He could hear them. He knew they were here to guide him. Instantly, he had a new plan.

He shouted for his men to wait there while he kicked his big gray dappled horse for the head of the line and Buffalo Horn. 'Take our people and go up that canyon,' he pointed, off to the right. 'The horse soldiers are climbing fast. I will take the rest of our warriors with me to lead them away from you. When you hear rifle fire, do

155

not stop or send help back to us. Keep going until you reach the top and go over into Canada land. I will meet you there later.'

Iron Hand turned to Manley and Story, who hadn't understood a word of Sioux but knew there was a sudden change in plans. 'You have served me well,' he leveled a gaze on both men. 'Once you cross the border you will be set free. Go now and do not stop.'

Both men stared back, only nodding as Kee-To reined his horse around and galloped back down the line of his people, gathering more warriors as he went. Reaching the band below, he raised his hand with a shout. 'Follow me, my brothers, and prepare for war!'

Half a mile up the valley, Kee-To split his braves into two parties opposite each other, hidden behind snow-covered terraces shouldering the shallow valley. He ordered warriors to let the horse soldiers ride in between them, catching them in a killing crossfire ambush. Gathering a dozen other braves, he rode back down to the entrance to the valley, pulling to a stop where the climbing horse soldiers could not miss seeing him.

'Kee-To, why do we wait here?' one brave questioned nervously.

'I want the soldiers to see me. Then they will follow us toward our brothers. We will lead them there like the wolf leads deer to slaughter.'

A snowy curtain of white raced down the slopes, beginning to envelop the land in a misty white fog. Stodlmeyer's scout, riding in the lead, looked up and pointed with a shout.

'Look, there they are, right up there!'

The colonel's pulse quickened. At long last he finally had the Sioux in sight and could close in on them. His face flushed red with anticipation while barking a command. 'Bugler, sound the charge!'

The horse soldiers began surging uphill behind Stodlmeyer, shouting and yelling while drawing pistols and pulling single-shot rifles out of bouncing scabbards.

Above, Kee-To still sat in the saddle without moving. '*Let them come closer,*' he thought to himself, while the braves around him looked on with growing alarm. Kicking their horses higher, the cavalrymen began firing their first shots while still too far away to hit, the bullets falling short in the snow. Kee-To watched them ride closer, the report of their rifles growing louder, until he finally gave the order to ride fast for the valley entrance.

When Stodlmeyer reached the point where he'd last seen the Sioux, he did not hesitate charging up the valley, shouting for his men to follow into the deathly ambush waiting ahead. Blinding snow and ice crystals stung their faces as a new wall of clouds swept down around them, cutting their vision to mere yards. Suddenly the welter of tracks changed to a big circle but in the instant it took for the colonel and his scout to realize what it meant it was already too late. Murderous rifle and pistol fire erupted close on both sides of the hapless cavalrymen, cutting them down like ripe wheat under the swing of a razor-sharp scythe. Cries of dying men were mixed with the whistling moan of wind, sounding like a devil's chorus leading the riders into a living hell. The colonel's horse reared straight up from bullet hits and fell, throwing him into the snow face first. He recovered, dragging himself up against the dying animal for cover, pulling his pistol and firing back blindly, while the deafening roar of weapons continued and more troopers tried to turn back but went down. The last thing Colonel Austin Vance Stodlmeyer ever saw was the Sioux on both sides rising to their feet and running in for final killing shots with pistols and rifles spitting fire.

Through the frantic scramble of death, Corporal Greenwood somehow remained unhit and alive. Head down, low in the saddle, he frantically dug spurs into his horse's side, charging through the slaughter and leaving the ambush scene behind. Kee-To saw him flash by. Leaping to his feet, he ran for his horse. Atop its back, he kicked away after the lone cavalryman. He wasn't going to let one single blue coat get away to tell the tale of what happened here.

Greenwood had no idea where he was going in the near white-out, he was only driven by the shivering fear he'd be caught and killed, too. He screamed at his horse to go faster, constantly digging cruel spurs into its heaving sides. Not far back, Iron Hand whipped his horse on for more speed, one hand on the reins, the other clutching a still-hot pistol. As both men rode higher, the clouds finally began to thin. For the first time, Kee-To could see Greenwood ahead of him. He screamed a war cry of victory, forcing the big gray under him on for even more speed. Greenwood looked back over his shoulder. His eyes grew wide in disbelief and his face twisted in agony. He stabbed for the pistol at his side. Pulling it, he fired back wildly over his shoulder, pulling the trigger again and again until the hammer fell on the sickening click of empty cylinders. Tossing the gun away, he pulled his head down low, cussing the animal to run faster.

Yard by yard, stride by stride, Kee-To's horse began closing the gap between the two men. Fifty yards shrank to thirty, twenty, ten. Then the two horses ran side by side. Kee-To pointed his pistol directly into the face of the terrified man, yet for some reason he did not fire. He'd seen that same kind of paralyzing fear on the faces of his own women, children and dying warriors all too often. Somehow it made him hesitate, trying to override his hatred of these white men and their wars upon him and all his people. His own sudden emotions stunned him. He wanted to kill this white man in the worst way, but still did not pull the trigger. Suddenly he turned the pistol ahead, firing a single shot into the neck of Greenwood's horse. The animal stumbled and fell, crashing to the ground. The corporal rolled away into the snow, before slowly pulling himself up to his knees and spitting out a mouthful of the cold white fluff, trying to suck in a breath of air. Kee-To dismounted quickly. Walking up to Greenwood, he stared down on the pathetic figure of the thoroughly beaten man. The pistol was still in his hands.

'Please . . . don't kill me . . . I'm begging you!' Greenwood pleaded, hands up, mouth quivering, looking into the black eyes of the Sioux chief. 'I never . . . killed any Sioux. You gotta . . . believe me, if you can understand . . . anything I'm saying. For God's sake, don't shoot!'

Kee-To didn't answer. Flashes of mixed emotions

played wildly across his mind even he could not under-stand. Suddenly he looked up beyond Greenwood to the final ridges of the Kicking Horse Mountains, barely a mile away. Canada and freedom lay just over those icy peaks. He looked farther down the ridges to the tiny figure of Buffalo Horn, leading his long line of people over that great divide. He'd promised all the Sioux tribes he'd bring them to safety this one last time, and now that promise was being fulfilled. He motioned with his pistol for Greenwood to get to his feet. Once standing, he gave the shivering man a final order.

'Go, and do not look back. Tell the horse soldiers my people are now free. Tell them the white man can never hold the Sioux. We are like the wind. You have closed your hand on nothing. Now we are gone.'

Greenwood stood staring back, mouth half open, as Kee-To, Iron Hand remounted his horse, pulling it around and starting for the ridges. The lowly corporal's life had been spared by the man who was supposed to be the most savage killer in the Sioux Nation. He still couldn't understand why. Maybe he never would, but he'd deliver that message of freedom to the generals and they'd ponder its meaning too for years to come. It was and is an ancient divide between two vastly different people that has never been bridged. It's likely it never will.